ARABELLA

Elizabeth Blake-Thomas

Table of Contents

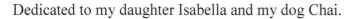

DEDICATION

Dedicated to my daughter Isabella and my dog Chai.

Thank you to my mum, my friends and everyone who has helped me on my journey from the beginning.

THE 'HAVE YOUR CAKE AND EAT IT' TRUST

Having experienced a divorce, one of the hardest things Elizabeth had to deal with was the financials. Not for her, but for her daughter. It was the little things that suddenly were difficult to pay for on a limited budget, like camps and courses, or birthday parties and cakes, presents at Christmas time for her daughter's teachers and friends. So, in order to help other single-parent families, she set up a foundation to help with the smaller financial issues that really matter to a child. If you feel you qualify or would like to make a donation to the "Have Your Cake and Eat It Fund", then please email Elizabeth at lizzie.bt@hotmail.co.uk.

Thanks

Elizabeth Blake Thomas
Director and Writer
www.elizabethblakethomas.com

THE WIZARD OF OZ

Dorothy: 'There's no place like home.'

It was late at night on yet another Saturday that Arabella didn't have a date. The old clock in the hallway chimed 9 pm with its long, slightly creaky sounding bells. It reminded Arabella of how she felt. Like a classic antique that didn't sound as good as it used to, but was just about standing strong. A clock that only a certain type of person might want to have at home before getting rid of it and replacing it with a newer, cheaper, skinnier looking version.

Arabella was incredibly beautiful in a weathered, having experienced life kind of way. She had long blonde hair, was 5ft 7 and slender. She had been told on more than one occasion that she radiated positive energy from her entire being. In her mid-thirties, she had lots of positive energy. This energy was usually taken up with the love of her life, her daughter, Lily. Arabella missed her only daughter so much, it ached. Having to share your child, (even if not very often) is the worst part of divorce, she thought.

Mark had made such a big deal about co-parenting and sharing responsibilities. Co-parenting to him meant only seeing Lily when it fitted in with his schedule as well as sending one email a month to "catch up". It wasn't very often that Lily actually visited Mark due to the number of parties and events he and Betty attended. Mark was tall, 6ft 2, suave in a greasy Italian looking kind of way. He was skinny but had a bit of a stomach. Betty was the "other woman" too predictable to describe, however for the benefit of everyone's imagination, she was tall, skinny, blonde and young. Classic affair material.

Arabella joked with her friends who had more than one child. They could lose one and still have one spare. But if she lost her daughter... well, she didn't even want to think about it. Of course, she hadn't lost Lily, when the separation proceedings had begun, she presumed she would get Lily full time and she was correct. She and Lily were a team. Arabella took her to all her extracurricular classes and made sure she had the best costumes for any of the school parades or plays. Lily knew she could count on her mum for anything and everything. Arabella had taught her how to ride her first bike, how to speak French and how to swim.

Arabella and Mark both agreed on the rules for "parent time." Each must be able to contact Lily whenever they pleased, whilst Lily was with the other parent. Seemed simple enough.

Especially as Lily was never really with Mark.

Arabella had experienced watching Lily on Facetime, at Mark's new home. It allowed Arabella to peek into his new world – a world he had infiltrated with such ease. He had told Arabella that Betty's parents were "wealthy, influential and important people." Translated as "A world of money, fast cars and a whole lot of bullshit." Lily once took her mother on a virtual tour of Betty's house. A house that was most certainly owned by Betty's parents and a place so grand Arabella wondered how could Mark possibly hope to contribute to such a lavish lifestyle. Mark enjoyed telling everyone that he gave half his salary in maintenance to Arabella. Always his excuse for having no money. Typical of Mark, exaggerating the truth. Lily had led Arabella into Betty's closet where she saw her countless Jimmy Choos lined up as if they were her precious children. All sitting, well-behaved, in rows, taken out when they suited Betty's day. Louis Vuitton littered the floor and Hermes scarves draped the mirrors.

Just then, Arabella spotted one of her ex-husband's bank statements on the side and asked Lily to retrieve it. (Truthfully, "on the side" meant "in a drawer and under another pile of papers.") Apparently, Mark had spent a considerable amount of money on wining and dining Betty, using more money he didn't actually have. This came as quite a shock, as he had not been able to contribute anything extra towards Lily that month. Arabella decided that snooping wasn't the healthiest option and so had chosen to no longer Facetime.

But tonight was different. Mark had taken Lily and his girlfriend to his neighbor's party.

Mark insisted Lily should be allowed to go to the party as her cousins and a number of other children would also be there. But Arabella knew this was just another excuse for Mark to play the role of the perfect dad. Mark enjoyed showing Lily off in all her glory. Almost like a circus monkey, she would perform for him when it suited his needs. Arabella would normally spend the weekend with Lily watching TV and eating chocolate. Mark had gone on and on about how important this party was and Arabella, not wanting to deprive her daughter of anything, eventually conceded.

Arabella promised Mark that she would turn the volume on the microphone down and only watch Lily socializing at the event. "If only I could have turned you down when we were married," Mark said.

Arabella forced a fake half-laugh, almost instantly regretting it.

The night of the party, Arabella watched through her phone as Lily and the kids played, danced and ran around. Seeing Lily having fun eased Arabella's conscience about the effects the separation might have had on her. As long as she knew Lily was happy, that was all that mattered.

Betty tolerated Lily, but as with most younger girlfriends, Arabella found that Betty's schedule didn't ever include her beloved daughter. On the odd occasion when Lily spent a daddy/daughter day with Mark, Betty incessantly called his phone. Eventually, Mark returned Betty's call and pacified her, cooing "No darling, I'm not ignoring you."

Couldn't Mark spend any time with his daughter without Betty's constant childlike interruptions? Arabella had a strong sense that Betty was desperate to have her own children with Mark. Which would explain Betty's lack of effort to make Lily feel loved and supported. Arabella couldn't wait for Betty to learn what Mark was really like when he had his own family. Sleepless nights, crying babies and baby-sick on her Gucci shoes. It wasn't that Mark was a totally bad person, he was just incredibly selfish. Mark's behavior consisted of staying out late with "the boys," drinking till beyond drunk and not taking his responsibilities seriously. He would forget special occasions. Arabella's routine for Lily was mocked by him and if an important family decision needed to be made it was always left till the last minute. He would create small arguments about things like housework and then much bigger arguments about financials. Money was always a bone of contention.

Mark wanted a very different way of life than Arabella. When Lily had arrived on the scene this had made the gap between them more obvious.

Arabella had grown up but Mark hadn't.

The gathering tonight was set in a beautiful old house, probably Victorian, although Arabella always got the styles confused. After browsing through home and design magazines, she attempted to recreate what she saw, but could never quite pull it off. Arabella's little cottage was cute. Nothing special, just cute.

This house, however, was filled with grandeur. Beautiful old bookcases and intricately carved side tables adorned the rooms. Huge windows stretched from floor to ceiling draped with large heavy curtains and a long table that could easily feed at least sixteen people. An open fire roared alongside. The house belonged to a celebrity who was a friend of the family. And everyone knew it. Mark was a shameless name dropper.

Arabella got a glass of water whilst watching Lily on the screen. As she turned back though, something caught her eye. Something flickered. Something red. Wait. Was that a flame? Arabella stared in horror as a mass of flames spread from the rug to the carpet and then engulfed the curtains. Arabella saw the panic in the children's eyes. She heard their screams as they pushed each other out of the way, desperate to leave. She finally spotted Lily rooted to the spot. Frozen.

Arabella screamed at her daughter to get out but she wasn't

responding. "Lily, get out! Run! Please!" Arabella, powerless, was at her wit's end. She watched as Lily, terrified and disorientated, curled herself into a ball and hid under the large wooden table. The fire continued to grow and the curtains continued to burn. Followed by the rest of the room. Arabella looked on helplessly as if in a scene from a movie. The one where you shout at the screen to warn someone they're about to get murdered but they still walk into the kitchen and get stabbed because they can't hear you.

Arabella, frantic, grabbed her car keys and her phone, dialed 999 and leapt into her car. She couldn't breathe. Her chest tightened. She knocked over the gatepost and flew off the curb. Nothing was stopping her from getting to that house. She didn't care about lights, traffic or the police. She had to get to Lily. What would she do without her? What would her life become?

Finally, she pulled up to the large gates. Cars, fire engines, and people were everywhere. She dashed to the door. The inside of the house was black, with smoke billowing out of doors and windows. People with limbs singed, crying and screaming in pain were fleeing for cover. The scene was reminiscent of a horror movie. The putrid smell of burning flesh caught in Arabella's throat. She immediately swayed to the side. Faint and sick and barely able to walk, she forced herself further into the house. Now familiar with the layout from her Facetime call with Lily earlier in the evening, she pressed on, shoving people out of the way. Arabella, hysterical, screamed out Lily's name repeatedly, unaware of anyone or anything around her.

"Lily! Mark! Lily?"

She caught sight of Mark and bolted towards her ex, who was

comforting his girlfriend in his arms.

"Where is our daughter? Where is she?" She shook Mark, shouting at him.

"I don't know," Mark answered, holding Betty.

Arabella ran into the sitting room, searching. There under the table, wrapped in a little ball, black and burnt was her baby. She wailed out in anguish as she held the body of her limp child and rocked her in her arms.

Arabella woke with a start, sweating and crying. She could never get to her baby. Mark had moved out and it plagued her sleeping hours. The nightmares had begun ever since.

Every night was filled with the same dream.

It was so crystal clear it scared her.

AMERICAN BEAUTY

Lester: "You don't get to tell me what to do ever again."
Ricky: "I'M not obsessing, I'M just curious."

Arabella was having a particularly difficult week. She was afraid to sleep, in case she was greeted with another nightmare, and today, like every morning recently, she felt in utter despair.

She just couldn't go on.

Her doctor assured her it would get easier and gave her "happy pills" to help her cope with the dark days that seemed to engulf her at every turn. She had seen how certain medication had affected a close friend. She didn't want to rely on them. So she refused to take them.

Where had it all gone wrong? What could she have done differently? These were the questions she asked herself every day. She exhaled deeply, dreading the day ahead. A sinking sensation, deep in the pit of her stomach refused to subside as she made her way to the bathroom. She reached inside the cabinet, the door still swinging on its hinges. Mark had never managed to fix it. Well, it certainly wasn't going to happen now, was it? Just like the broken banister, the glass panel in the kitchen and the broken bed in Lily's room! All of those DIY jobs were reminders of her past life. A life that was now tainted.

Arabella, almost cadaverous, gazed at her ashen self in the mirror. The mirror really should have been cleaned, although the dirtier it was the less she could see of herself. She reached forward with the hand towel and smeared the dirt around and around.

She had aged so much in the last year. There were definitely more wrinkles than yesterday. She peered at her reflection and counted each one; yep two more. She pulled her face back like a Madonna facelift and pursed her lips in a glorious pout. She lifted her arms up; yep, that bag of crisps from last night had appeared! She checked her knees, they were definitely wrinklier too. Life was cruel, but at least she wasn't going gray, a small mercy to be thankful for. After reading an article on the loo about aging, she had studied her pubic area and did happen to find one gray hair. It had been particularly painful to remove, but well worth it. Even if it was just herself that admired the view from now on.

Bet 'Miss Perfect' doesn't have anything wrinkly yet.

I must not compare myself to her.

Another helpful quote from Jeremy Kyle. Increasingly lethargic, she threw cold water on her face, barely brushed her teeth and hair and half-heartedly attempted to shut the cabinet. She would try without the pills again today.

The self-help books said a divorce could take at least a couple of years to get over. She had laughed at this and thought that was way too long but they were right, she was still feeling like crap and apparently only half way through.

"How to Get Through Divorce...." Easy to understand, she thought, as it had the simplest title. She ticked off the emotions as she went through them. "You will experience, guilt, then anger, followed by resentment. She had forgotten which one she was up to

and what she should be feeling right now. It was too overwhelming.

She walked down the narrow hallway of the sweet little Shakespearean style cottage, past an ever-growing pile of washing.

Lily's toys and books were strewn across the stairs too. Tidying had been one of Arabella's strong points. It was the domestic thing she was excellent at. The house had always been immaculate. Now, her home reflected her present state of mind. A total and utter jumble of stuff.

She dodged the messy items beautifully. Like an ice skater performing her piece in front of the judges. She walked past an empty wall with faded areas where photos and paintings had previously hung. Arabella couldn't face replacing the space with anything else quite yet. Photos of the family meant so much to her, the family wall. The bare walls seemed to mirror her empty heart and she found a slight solace in that.

She ambled into the open-plan kitchen. It was small but perfectly shaped to accommodate family breakfasts and visitors who loved sitting and chatting. She made a cup of tea and feebly attempted to haul herself out of the negative place she had woken up in. She remembered the words of her therapist again, who told her to find her "happy" place. She wasn't sure where that was yet. She still had to find a replacement.

Lulled for some time by the water bubble as the kettle boiled, she eventually reached for her phone and saw the dreaded red notification number flashing at her. Each night she would go to bed with a clear phone but every morning she would wake up to more messages and countless emails from Mark. That dreaded flashing red number sitting there in its little red circle. Damn that little red circle, did Apple know what this did to her?

Another day of harassment, I can't deal with this right now.

She turned her phone on silent and flipped it over.

I just need a few more minutes.

The little cottage was particularly quiet as Lily was on a sleepover at her best friend's. Up until the last month or so, Lily had never been on sleepovers. So this had been a really big deal for them both. *She is too young*, Arabella had thought. *She needs her sleep.* Or maybe it was more about Arabella needing her sleep. The horror stories that came back from parents saying their children hadn't fallen asleep until three in the morning or worse still, they had stayed awake all night. But ever since Arabella needed time off from being the happy parent in front of Lily, her best friend Nicki had been good enough to offer her home as respite.

Arabella and Nicki had grown up together so she trusted her with her life. Lily was also best friends with Nicki's daughter Olivia, so it really worked out well. Nicki lived just down the road in a similarly styled cottage with a lovely husband and they had all been good friends. In fact, the village seemed to welcome a close knit community. You knew that no matter what happened, you could call on each other if you had locked yourself out of your house or if you just wanted to borrow some milk or sugar.

The great thing about not having Lily this morning meant that Arabella could spend a few moments imagining everything was normal. She often allowed herself this somewhat distorted pleasure. If she closed her eyes and drifted off into an alternate reality, she could find the means to cope.

She imagined her husband still upstairs in their big comfy white company-style bed whilst she snuck downstairs to make breakfast and tea for him. He loved Earl Grey, a rather limp drink, but Arabella thought it was endearing, especially as he drank it from a cup Lily had made for him. A pink cup, marked with Lily's handprints and birth date that she designed herself, along with a matching plate and bowl.

Arabella would lovingly place slices of warm buttery toast with poached eggs on top and pour freshly squeezed orange juice. She'd creep past Lily's bedroom, so as not to wake her and crawl back into her husband's bed. She'd entwine her legs around his, locking him close. She'd hated him leaving even if it was because he needed to go to work and he, in turn, had loved that she desired him to stay. He'd kiss her neck, rub her shoulders and look deep into her eyes. Hold her in his arms and tell her he loved her. She'd asked how much, and he'd said: "To the moon and back."

It was their thing.

The tray would fall to the floor like in *Fifty Shades of Gray* and passion raucously ensued. They knew they had to make love quickly before Lily woke up.

The neighbor's dogs barking incessantly brought Arabella back to earth with a hollow thud. Lost in thought, she aimlessly pulled out two mugs, realizing that the one Lily had made for her Daddy was still there. He hadn't taken it. She wondered what cup he was drinking his tea out of this morning. Would he be at Betty's? Would he be going out for breakfast or eating in? He insisted he had no intention of living with Betty but as far as Arabella knew Mark had moved in with her months ago. What did it matter? Ten months had gone by. It didn't matter what she knew or didn't know. He had made it very clear that he was now living his life.

She sat down and turned her phone over, the countless notifications glaring back at her.

Arabella wasn't sure how much more she could take. Another five emails? Twenty texts? Did no-one know what Mark was really like? Could no-one see through his niceness? What originally had attracted Arabella to Mark, his suave British mannerisms, now made her blood boil. He had a Colin Firthiness about him.

From time to time people stopped him in the street, confusing him for one famous British actor or another, which he of course lapped up like an excitable puppy. Mark loved to think he was more upper class than he actually was, but because Arabella had loved him so much she tended to look past this oddity. She also turned a blind eye to his forgetfulness, his lack of consideration for anyone other than himself, and the fact he had to be reminded about birthdays and special occasions. Every single one.

When they had first met, Arabella had loved spoiling Mark. She bought him gifts galore, took him out and on his birthday, arranged surprise birthday parties for him. She always thought that she would marry an older man which made her relationship with Mark unexpected and exciting.

At first she was enamored by the thought of marriage, big houses, cars and private schools for their children, but that soon changed. She met a whole new crowd of people once she left university, giving her an insight into young, fun, carefree and penniless graduates. They all wanted to be lawyers and were practicing at a firm in London. They seemed to love their jobs but also knew how to party and make the most of life outside of work. Arabella thought this might be a profession she would enjoy and applied for a job as an intern over the summer to get work experience. She turned up to the office that first day not knowing what to expect. A little frazzled, like a deer caught in headlights. She wore tight black leather trousers and a green jumper. She cringed when she thought back on it. However Mark was immediately attracted to her when they were introduced, so she couldn't have looked that bad.

Within the first few days of Arabella's new job, they began seeing each other. They kept it a secret from the rest of the office in case it made things awkward but before long, they started officially dating and once she finished her summer job with the firm it was common knowledge they were a couple. Arabella, convinced he was the one, started to plan their wedding. Things didn't go completely according to said plan as Arabella gave birth to Lily before the arranged wedding date but still, she couldn't have been any happier. Lily was now not only a reason for the celebrations but also part of them.

They were the perfect trio.

Family and friends gathered for a huge wedding party. Arabella had spent months planning the perfect day. She specifically chose the colours and even made all the table decorations. Arabella wanted Mark to feel part of the occasion so she asked him to arrange the music for their first dance. A beautiful song that they'd chosen together. On the wedding day, when it came to giving the DJ the song, Mark forgot it.

HE FORGOT IT!

Arabella was heartbroken. She felt so let down. The best man quickly had to run to the nearest music store and purchase the CD. Then on his return, the song was played but it was the wrong version. It was the Elton John version as opposed to Moulin Rouge. Arabella remembered dancing with Mark but feeling so upset that he hadn't cared enough to remember this. So much for her perfect day.

Now, ten years later and eight years of marriage, they were coming to the end of a long acrimonious separation. Perhaps she should have seen it coming but this was most certainly not where she expected to be right now. Mark had always been self-centered, but she had been too in love to notice.

She craved doing something creative. Working at the law firm had been fun for a while, but she knew her career path was veering off completely. Mark, terribly unsure of who he was and what he truly wanted, could be difficult to live with.

First, he wanted Arabella to be a stay at home mum but then he would get extremely jealous when Arabella and Lily went off on play dates and school trips abroad. Ultimately Mark realized that if he was the only one working he could control Arabella financially. Then he would suddenly complain Arabella did nothing and earned nothing.

She couldn't win.

Another beep. Dammit! She knew she couldn't ignore her phone for much longer. She begrudgingly looked back over her text messages from Mark, which were laced with anger and now always full of blame.

"You have completely ruined everything for yourself."

What on earth was he talking about? As far as she was concerned, things couldn't get much worse. She had almost no money as the financials weren't finalized, no husband, no job prospects because she couldn't afford the child care, and voila, last night she spotted two extra wrinkles.

She couldn't afford to do a proper food shop until her monthly allowance came in so she had eaten dry pasta, crisps, and frozen fruit for supper the night before. Money had always been tight but now Mark was paying for his girlfriend, living a lifestyle that was expected of him, which didn't leave much over for Arabella and Lily. Holidays abroad and regular visits to Jimmy Choo and Louis Vuitton meant he was "hard up" most months.

Arabella would laugh out loud at how materialistic and broke Mark could be at the same time. That is, until she was faced with the moments where she couldn't afford to do the most basic of things with Lily.

She really wanted to believe Mark would be different and ensure Lily was always cared for. His parents had divorced and he would tell Arabella how hard it had been for his mother. Could Arabella have been any more wrong? Her own mother offered to help, but Arabella declined her kind proposal. It was Mark's responsibility to take care of Lily and he needed to come to terms with that. Arabella's mother adored Lily and spoiled her whenever she could.

Arabella looked out of the kitchen cottage window eying a small vegetable garden that she'd cultivated. She imagined herself living a hippy lifestyle, eating her own produce, selling the leftovers, even making her own clothes.

She could see it right now. Her and Lily entirely self-sufficient. Okay, maybe that was a step too far as she couldn't even sew on a button, but you get the picture. Home had always been an important place for Arabella. A place for her daughter, where she felt safe and secure. She believed home could be anywhere though and it wasn't about the bricks and mortar, it was wherever the love was. Lily's room was covered in adorable little fairy lights, with a magic reading area that Lily and Arabella loved to escape to. They hid there at night and pretended they were locked away in a tower with only each other as company. If they weren't well behaved they would be trapped forever.

Arabella improvised, making up stories for Lily and then writing them down later so she could tell them to her whenever she wanted to hear them. "Tell me the one about the dragon again Mummy." Lily often said. This was how Arabella had found that she loved creating stories and it became more and more therapeutic as time went on. The stories turned into her thoughts which turned into a diary. She realized she loved writing.

Lily too, showed a real skill for storytelling and clearly had a wondrous imagination. They sat for hours with puppets and cushions, making up scenes. Arabella adored escaping into Lily's fantasy world, reveling in the freedom of it all. After all, she'd often disappear into her own fantasy world. Arabella couldn't imagine moving and bringing Lily up anywhere else, but she knew things were about to change and she needed to start preparing for this possibility. She walked over to the record player and put on Bing Crosby. *He was a good man*, Arabella thought.

She looked through the slightly frosted window, watching the autumn leaves fall from the tree, Bing crooning as if to her personally. She had so much to be grateful for, and sometimes she needed reminding of this. Arabella had considered putting an end to it all after she had discovered Mark's affair. She didn't think she could ever recover from the pain and the humiliation. Her mind had lost the feeling of normality, she could no longer function and had felt totally abandoned.

When she felt at rock bottom she discovered a way to cope; she would picture Lily's angelic face and bright smile and this was enough to jolt her from the depths of depression. A thought flashed through her mind of an older Lily discussing how hard life was without a mother on one of those awful agony aunt TV shows.

"So Lily, why do you think your mother killed herself? Were you too much for her? Didn't she love you at all?"

Arabella snapped out of it. No matter how awful she felt, she couldn't do that to Lily. She would start by focusing on each day, not worrying about tomorrow but thinking about the here and now. Ten months was enough time to feel this deep dark depression.

What other small changes could she make? She read yesterday that if you can focus on the next twenty-four hours then it will lead into the next and so on. Before you realize it you will have made it through a week, then a month. This is what she was attempting to do today. She could start by sorting out the cupboards or perhaps clean out some of Lily's things. It was a start.

Arabella's group of friends had been incredibly supportive this last year, always offering to help out with anything and everything. The motley crew consisted of Arabella's school mates Julie and Nicki, and Jen and Alice who joined the group when they moved into the area with children the same age as Lily. Each week they got together for "book club". Book club might as well have been code words for an agony aunt crisis circle with some village gossip thrown in for good measure, as none of them ever actually read the books. They took it in turns, going to each other's houses and arrived with plenty of tea and biscuits. Sometimes something stronger was also called for. They chatted and laughed for hours. She didn't think she could have survived this ordeal without her friends. They had been her lifeline.

In the beginning, the affair was such a shock to not only Arabella but to all her friends. She was a mess and everything was a blur. The stress caused her memory to forget everything. Her friends rallied around, creating a rota, making sure there was someone to collect Lily, make supper and check on Arabella, who would constantly forget to eat and drink. Bit by bit, she started to pull herself together and her friends let her be once they could see she could at least function with the day-to-day things.

Arabella grabbed her phone. Something hit her, a strong feeling of "enough is enough". She could do more than just tidy up. She could do a total cleanse. Maybe this was the push she needed. She texted -

Book club at mine tonight! 7.30 pm, don't be late.

She felt a little better already. *One small step* she told herself. She must get dressed, wear something to make her feel good. Another book had said, "If your clothes don't bring you joy then don't wear them". There was a problem. It meant she had nothing to wear. Her clothes definitely didn't bring her joy, they didn't fit her and definitely didn't fit in with her lifestyle, considering she hadn't had a life this last year.

Nicki had a great eye for fashion, maybe she would help Arabella. She wondered if her body was also due a revamp but Arabella despised exercise. The sweating, the heat and the pain, she could definitely do without. *I'll hardly eat*, she thought. *Then I'll never have to exercise again.*

Her mind started to drift. Should she go on a retreat like Julia Roberts in *Eat, Pray, Love*? Arabella imagined herself in Italy looking out across the long warm vineyards, cooking (or at least holding some garlic and rubbing it into some other food) and meeting gorgeous dark Italian men. They sauntered up to her, peering down over their sunglasses as she sat in a floaty kaftan, wearing a black wide-brimmed hat like in that Alex Katz painting. She would be deep into working on her latest novel. They would approach her, telling her how wonderful it was to have a sexy woman who could cook and write. As she started to look up towards the men from under her large brim she stood up as if to kiss them when…

BANG!

She hit her head on the cupboard door that was left open.

She hurried upstairs to start on her closet. Yes, this was what she needed, an emotional and practical declutter. As she turned to look at all her 'things', she wondered how her life would be if she didn't have 'things?' Julia Roberts probably doesn't have "things" What if she simplified her life? I mean, why the heck was she keeping broken Christmas decorations, clothes that didn't fit, and church service sheets from other people's weddings? Arabella had an epiphany. She didn't need things... they were just holding her back! She snatched her phone and continued to text.

No reading tonight ladies, it's time to sort. Come and help yourself to some of my stuff. I've decided to get rid. A small step for man but a huge step for Arabella.

BACK TO THE FUTURE

Marty: "If you put your mind to it, you can accomplish anything."

The idea always seemed a good one in the beginning. Where would she start? How on earth did she end up with so much stuff? This had seemed like such a good idea an hour ago. The room was now totally covered. She knew she didn't have nearly as much as some of her friends, but she still managed to fill every cupboard, every box on every shelf and every little bit of space in every box. She kept all of Lily's old school work and every single note Lily had ever given to her. There was a piece of paper with what could only be described as a scribble, but it was Lily's first scribble so she could never get rid of it. And the note that just read "LOVE…" At nursery, they asked Lily to write down her favourite word. How could she ever get rid of that?

Arabella remembered seeing one of those Pinterest boards, "How to store precious childhood memories", but you had to be brutal and clear things first and every time she had gone to throw something away, she couldn't go through with it. Not surprisingly, the pile hadn't gone down at all. It had just moved from one side of the room to the other.

Arabella wondered if there might be a reason she was so reluctant to get rid of her stuff. Perhaps the stuff was not the problem. Perhaps it was what it represented. The end of an era, the end of her baby being a baby and life moving on. She remembered reading something about that in one of her other self-help books. She felt saddened by this.

This clear out was supposed to make her feel good, not remind her of the past. She was now surrounded by clothes, shoes, toys, blankets and old presents - the list went on. There were even items that still had the sale tags attached. This stuff must be worth something to someone. What if she sold most of her things that had no sentimental value and then she could use the money to fund a mini-adventure for her and Lily? A Christmas trip? She started to cheer up, imagining herself on a desert island, or maybe in Paris taking in the sights. She could even buy herself a real Hermes scarf…

Hold on there, lady! She was trying to get rid of stuff, not buy more!

She grabbed her phone as she remembered Julie was having a car boot sale this weekend. Maybe she could tag along and sell her stuff too?

Under a pile of Lily's old clothes, which she couldn't help but pick up and smell, the baby smell that had actually turned musty, she saw the last photo album she had created when they had all been together. The three of them loved travelling and each time they returned, she would get all the photos developed and sit for hours arranging the album. With Mark so busy at work they hadn't been on a trip for a very long time. Their last family trip had been to the South of France. They had wandered through the markets, tasting olives and later riding bikes along the coast. Lily was only a baby at the time so they had found a bike with a seat and spent hours exploring, accompanied by a baguette and fresh olives picked from the market. That was one of Mark's favourite things to do, purchase fresh olives from European markets. They stretched out alongside the rivers, away from the hustle and bustle of the town and talked and talked, planning their future. The South of France felt like her spiritual home. A bit like that Woody Allen movie, *Magic in the Moonlight*. She had always felt like she was from a different era and a different city. Yes, maybe this was the answer. Arabella and Lily could get a fresh perspective travelling somewhere new and exciting! She ran downstairs and grabbed her computer.

Christmas destinations for single mums, she typed.

Wow, it was a lot more expensive than she remembered. Flight, car, and accommodation cost as much as a couple of pairs of Betty's Jimmy Choos. How about just flight and accommodation? Still too expensive. Must be because it's Christmas.

OK, rethink. What if she went and stayed with people she knew? Friends or family? She didn't fancy Blackpool where Aunty Doreen lived, that's for sure. The south coast was an option but it was freezing and wouldn't feel like much of a holiday. No, it had to be somewhere further away. Somewhere hot. A picture of St Bart's appeared on the screen. White beaches and warm waters, perfect for that Christmas getaway. She imagined herself dipping her feet in the water and Lily making sand castles nearby. The thought of fleeing to anywhere afar, even for a few moments, lifted Arabella's spirits. She felt free and alive for the first time in months! She imagined Mark, dressed in rags, returning to an abandoned home, suddenly realizing he had made a mistake. Arabella had no idea why he would be dressed like a homeless person but it was her daydream so she'd dress him as she pleased!

He'd knock on the door, running in shouting "Scarlet, Scarlet, Miss O'Hara where are you? Am I too late?" Oh, wait… this wasn't her dream but a scene from *Gone with the Wind*. OK, so maybe she hadn't actually gone away and instead was just about to leave. Mark would run in shouting, "Arabella, Arabella, am I too late? Please don't go, what will I do without you?" and she would turn with her suitcase and say, "Frankly my dear I don't give a damn" and walk out.

She smiled. She treasured those precious moments where she could escape the harsh realities of the journey she had been forced to go on. An escape into her favourite films and musicals. She would get this far away look that took her to a safe place, a different character. It was a coping mechanism that Arabella had taught herself when things had been at their lowest. Instead, she was forced to take a journey she hadn't quite been ready to take.

She had a right to fantasize.

And fantasize she would.

Even though Mark and Arabella supposedly shared their daughter, Lily essentially lived with her. Arabella attempted to encourage a good relationship with Lily and her father, but Lily remained uninterested. She was still deeply hurt by her father's affair and the lies he had told her. Mark initially had tried to blame Arabella for his affair but as time went on he made less and less attempts to ease Lily's pain. He was currently spending the time forcing Betty onto Lily. Supposedly he had visited a counselor ("one of the best!") and she had instructed him to push Betty into Lily's life. The counselor knew nothing about Lily and what she was going through. It would happen when Lily was ready. Just because Mark felt the time was right for him did not mean the time was right for Lily.

Screaming and floods of tears followed whenever Arabella mentioned "Daddy". Lily's reaction had initially been a surprise to Arabella, but with another woman in the picture, she understood Lily's reluctance. Separation which was naturally leading to divorce was never easy. She had been told that a million times by her friends and even random strangers, but Arabella had no idea what that really meant, until now. Arabella truly hoped Lily's hatred for her father would eventually dissipate as time went on. She tried to get Lily to call him, meet up with him, even just an email. Every time there was a huge scene. It had proved too much for Mark, who wanted a much easier life and had imagined this would have been simpler and more textbook perfect.

Betty meet Lily, your new step mum.

(Hugs and soaring music begins)

But nope, that didn't look like it was ever going to be on the cards.

Arabella returned to her computer and immediately an advert for Hawaii grabbed her attention. Ooooh yes, she had always wanted to go there! White beaches, clear warm waters, good-looking surfers. She gazed out of the window and far into the distance. She saw herself drinking champagne on an isolated beach, surrounded by gorgeous male models. As she finished off a cocktail by the hotel pool, she eyed a lounger beside her, empty. Perhaps Pierce Brosnan, Brad Pitt or Bradley Cooper would fill it, she thought. She tasted the fresh watermelon in her mouth and saw her legs stretched out in front of her, beautifully tanned and slender. She felt a pair of hands rub her shoulders, soothing her taut muscles.

"Arabella," she heard her name called. "Arabella."

"Yes, I will have another freshly squeezed kiwi juice please," Arabella said. She looked round and… Oh bugger! Arabella was suddenly brought back to reality with a mighty THUMP. She hadn't noticed the front door open and a little person calling to her in the hallway. It was Lily. She practically jumped onto Arabella's lap.

"Did you have fun having a sleepover?"

"Yes, but I missed you, Arabella."

Lily was going through the phase where she called everyone by their first name. It all began because Arabella had started referring to Mark as "Idiot" and "Plonker". A very un-mummy like thing to do, which Arabella felt awful about. Unfortunately, Lily soon followed suit so Arabella quickly went back to "Mark." Your Daddy is not an idiot. Your Daddy is not a plonker, Arabella reminded herself. Perhaps if she said it enough times she would actually believe it.

"I missed you too."

Lily grabbed Arabella and whispered, "I love you Arabella" in her ear. Now this was heaven. An unparalleled precious moment. Nothing could take this away from her. Lily looked up and saw the computer.

"What are you doing, Arabella?"

"I'm looking at holiday places my darling, for us to go to this

Christmas. I think it's time for a trip, don't you?"

"Holiday, yay!"

"How about Hawaii?"

"Maybe."

"OK, what about New York?"

"Uh, maybe."

"Iran?"

"Maybe."

Arabella quickly realized Lily had no real idea of where she wanted to go.

"Los Angeles?"

Lily's face beamed back at Arabella.

"Arabella, I don't mind where we go as long as I'm with you forever and ever."

Another phase Lily was going through was that she wanted to be with Arabella 24/7. She even asked if she could marry her yesterday.

'Arabella, can I marry you?"

"Honey, you won't want to marry your mummy when you're older."

Lily, crushed, hung her head in disappointment. Arabella changed tactics.

"Of course you can, my darling."

Marriage was a funny thing. It was supposed to be for life, yet life sometimes got in the way. She knew she and Mark were meant to be together from the very beginning. It had just felt right. The moment she had laid her eyes on him. He had looked across the room at Arabella and it was obvious that he had felt the same as she did. They had been sent off on a lunch run together on her first day in the office. Over the double macchiatos and paninis for the rest of the office, they had planned a date that night and that was it. The next couple of years had whizzed by.

The news of Lily came as a total shock to them both. Mark was less excited than Arabella. In fact, he took quite a few months to get used to the idea. Arabella knew though, like most things with Mark, that it might take time for him to realize this was the best thing since "sliced bread".

Arabella suggested they needed to find a proper place to live, perhaps a place to buy, so off they went in search of their perfect home. Not far from London was their first choice so that Mark could still commute to work easily. They found a cute village called Little Cocklesford. A picturesque cottage that only had two bedrooms but it was enough, enough for them to bring up their child and have a garden for her or him to play in. She remembered feeling so grateful they could afford this place. She wanted to make it as perfect as possible for them and so immediately started to plan furniture and décor. Her ex-mother-in-law had been so helpful as well. Offering to repaint and fix things - knowing Mark wasn't the best at DIY.

She remembered when they signed for the place, their first home. Arabella had never felt happier. She thought about the word 'happiness'. Maybe that was her happy place, this house, those memories. Falling pregnant was happiness, right? No matter what transpired as the years went on, this little person was always going to love you.

Pure, unadulterated joy.

Giving birth, however, could definitely not be described as happiness. She thought back to the hospital. It was so excruciatingly painful. Arabella was in labour for two days, with no drugs, continually screaming her lungs out. She heard them say, "There's the head." Well, surely it couldn't get any worse. But then came the shoulders, and Arabella thought she might actually pass out from the pain. Why hadn't she taken any drugs? When Lily finally arrived (on time, just like her mother) she was breathtakingly beautiful. Mark handed Lily to Arabella and introduced her straight away. "Here's Lily."

They all sat there together, exhausted but content. They were a real family. The magical three.

Arabella continued looking through the website with information about Los Angeles. All the celebs lived there! And Christmas in LA looked amazing. Rodeo Drive in Beverly Hills had its own tree. Santa Monica had lights and an ice skating rink near the beach. There was even a Father Christmas at a place called The Grove. Obviously there wouldn't be snow, but if they made it as Christmassy as they could, the change might be exactly what they needed. Christmas last year in the snow had been such disaster, Lily could do with a fresh set of memories. Arabella hated the snow anyway. Why would anyone like to get cold and wet? She loved the sun, which made LA the perfect choice.

Arabella searched through hotels and houses and imagined what it would be like to wake up in sunshine all day, every day. Perhaps Lily would love living by the beach too. Arabella's mind began to wander again. Maybe it was more than a holiday they needed but a complete change of scenery. She had considered living by the coast in the UK at one stage, but the weather was so unpredictable. Arabella's heart started beating at a rapid rate and then something wonderful happened.

She smiled.

A real smile.

A smile that said 'leave me here on this beach to enjoy the sun'. She saw what her and Lily's future looked like without the constant reminder of what she had lost to another woman. It was so cliché. She was a cliché ex-wife. She was sure Betty thought she was the cliché horrendous ex-wife. It appeared to Arabella that any man was going to say their ex-wife was deemed horrendous, that's why they're an ex-wife!

Last New Year…

How dare he! How dare he sit there across from her with that look on his face. A look of pure satisfaction. Yes, he had lost weight, was going grey, and still he managed to look at her with an "I'm the cat that got the cream and I'm doing better without you," expression plastered on his face. He was so annoyingly smug. The captain of smugness. Mr. Smug from Smugland.

Arabella, sick to her stomach, slowly got up, her blood running, rushing through her veins. It was fight or flight. She pulled back her arm, fist clenched and came at him with such a speed it took him completely by surprise, landing full-frontal on his nose. His head bounced back in shock. A bit like Hugh Grant in *Bridget Jones*; she could hear in her head the words "A fight, a real fight." He was bleeding, bleeding everywhere. The whole restaurant stared at her. Arabella got up, picked up Mark's glass of red wine and threw it in his face.

"Don't ever contact me again," she sobbed and walked out of the restaurant. The restaurant patrons clapped loudly as she curtsied and then left.

And now… the REAL last new year…

"How do you know?" were the words that brought her straight back to reality and reminded her she was in fact, not Bridget Jones.

He sat there, his precious nose still intact, but still looking smugger than smug. How did she know? Is that all he had to say? When she found out two weeks ago she had written him a long rambling letter. It was filled with all her emotions. It had her heart laid out bare, it explained the trauma she had gone through, and in response, that's all the bastard had to say? She remembered when it all started, when she had found out what he had been up to.

Last Christmas…

The best way to describe it was that it was like a scene from the film, *Sliding Doors*. You know, the scene where Gwyneth Paltrow comes back and sees her husband in bed with another woman or in the parallel scene, where she doesn't find him with another woman and he gets away with it.

But she ends up in the same place anyway.

It happened just like that. Arabella was scheduled to go into hospital for cancer cell removal, it wasn't serious enough to be life threatening but it was serious to go in and have it removed as soon as possible. She got regular check-ups like she was supposed to, but her results had recently become a concern. She ignored it for as long as she could but Mark insisted she needed to do something about it. She made the appointment for a time when Mark was certain to be around and Lily could be cared for. He was working such a lot recently. He spent late nights at the office and dined out with clients and Arabella didn't want to be a burden. Everything now arranged, the dreaded day arrived. Driving to the hospital, her phone rang.

"Hello."

"Hi, Arabella?"

"Yes."

"It's Dr. Sung. I'm sorry to have to do this but unfortunately, I have to cancel today. I have an emergency. We are going to have to reschedule."

Arabella, slightly bemused, sat thinking about the phone call. When did a doctor ever call up and cancel an operation? She had planned their entire Christmas around this operation. It was all arranged, everything was planned for. She knew Lily no longer believed in Father Christmas and she wanted to make sure the magic lived on, regardless. So she had thought about everything meticulously. She hadn't wanted a repeat of the year before...

Arabella thought back to the Christmas the previous year, when she was sick with the flu. Not the man flu but the real "Oh dear God, I'm literally going to die" flu.

The doctor said, "It will take at least a couple of weeks to recover."

"But it's Christmas!" Arabella responded, feeling completely dejected.

The doctor stared back, silent.

"It's Christmas," she replied again, weakly.

Still no response.

Lily was the priority and Arabella loved making it special for her. Mark always left her to organize the festivities. This last week was crucial in final preparations. What about the food shopping? And the cookies and carrots for Santa? Who would wrap the last gifts? It was going to be like *The Grinch who stole Christmas*. This can't be happening!

"I'm afraid you need to go to bed and stay there," the doctor said sternly. Mark looked positively petrified when Arabella relayed the information to him later that evening.

Arabella lay in bed that night, mentally working through what still needed to be done. Collect turkey, leave out cookies for Santa, and buy carrots for Rudolf. As she continued going through her list, she started to cry. She knew what was going to happen. Christmas was going to be a disaster!

She was right. Mark called his parents and told them there was no food. He forgot to put anything out for Santa and the presents were left unwrapped. Suddenly, it all became crystal clear. This man was totally incapable.

That flu Christmas had been a huge failure and Arabella vowed it would never happen again. So back to last Christmas. She made sure all preparations were completed way ahead of schedule. She also wanted to take any pressure off Mark as the poor man had been working so hard.

"Arabella, are you there? We will need to rearrange."

"Oh," was all Arabella could manage. She had mentally prepared herself for the operation. Mark had taken time off work to help out. Arabella was unsure if there would be another suitable time.

Arabella put down her phone, turned to Mark and spoke calmly.

"It's not happening today. Can you take me home, please?"

It was one of those beautiful pre-Christmas Eve days when everyone was full of the Christmas spirit. Lily was sitting in the back of the car singing Christmas songs to herself and the village looked as if it was plucked from a Christmas book.

"You OK about this?"

"Yes, I suppose, I just wasn't prepared for it not happening."

"Maybe it's good, you can't always be prepared for everything."

Arabella felt Mark was talking about something other than her operation but told herself to not be so silly.

"Just drop me off at the end of our drive, I want to collect some holly and bits for our displays."

"You sure you're going to be Ok?"

"Yes, don't worry about me, I'll be fine. I need to get back into arranging Christmas."

"Alright, as long as you're sure? We can come home too?"

"No, carry on for Lily's sake, she was so looking forward to getting all the last bits for the Christmas play she has arranged for us. I don't want to let her down."

"Love you, Mummy," Lily shouted from the car as they drove

away.

Arabella called Alice immediately, she needed some reassurance.

"It just seems so bizarre that the appointment was cancelled."

"I'm sure it's happened for a reason darling, just relax and enjoy this time off, you totally deserve it. Everything happens for a reason."

Alice was one of those spiritual hippies who worked "in the industry" as a costume designer. Arabella and Alice had been friends for years; they were godparents to each other's children and swore they would be friends forever.

"I have to go. I have to…yes I'm coming, no tell Brad that's not what I wanted him to wear…"

Not Brad Pitt but a local actor who was performing in the Christmas panto in the village hall. The little village had been a hive of activity, with locals baking and decorating and generally getting ready for the Christmas fair and panto.

The phone went dead. Arabella let out a huge sigh. Alice was right, maybe this happened for a reason. She could do something productive and sort out things she had put off throughout the year. She didn't know why, but the anxiety she felt all week was now escalating and she just couldn't seem to settle. She had presumed it was about her surgery but now that it was cancelled the anxiety was still there. Was she anxious about Christmas? No, at least she didn't think so.

Arabella decided fresh air might do her some good and walked down their drive collecting holly and berries as she went. She saw her neighbour and shouted, "Happy Christmas!"

"You watch yourself, deary. It's going to be a cold one tonight."

Mrs. Deary, as they liked to call her because she always called everyone deary and only spoke about the weather, was a sweet old lady. She had probably lived in the neighborhood all her life. People who moved in to the village didn't tend to leave.

Arabella opened the door of the cottage and noticed the handle didn't work properly. She would have to get Mark to deal with that later. Of course, she had asked him several times already but he had been so busy at work, it had slipped his mind, again.

She made her way into the kitchen, still feeling uneasy, and grabbed a glass of water. Sitting on the comfy sofa in the sitting room, she had a perfect view out over the garden. It was getting gray and dark outside. Arabella was so affected by the weather, she was convinced she had (SD) SAD. Self-diagnosed Seasonal Affective Disorder. Lily was so excitable over Christmas that Arabella could just about cope with December but it was January and the next few months that were always the worst. The months waiting in anticipation for spring. So that the New Year didn't seem so daunting, Arabella planned to start writing during Christmas. She was approached by a local book store owner who heard her reading one of her stories to Lily one day in the back of the store.

"Sorry to bother you but are you reading one of our books?"

"No, I'm not. Sorry, we can go, we just love sitting here."

"Please enjoy! I've been listening to you and I adore the story. It would be wonderful if we had it in the store."

"No, Mummy made the story up for me."

"Well, she's a very clever Mummy indeed."

Arabella decided that now was as good a time as any to start. She had bought herself a dark red leather-bound book to begin her writing. She wanted to keep her writing a secret from Mark until it was actually published. She was sure he would be so proud. Where did she put her writing book again? Arabella couldn't remember where she hid it. This wasn't like her, she must have been distracted with the impending hospital visit. She knew she had placed it somewhere safe. Lily tended to find anything Arabella had bought for herself to draw in. Normally Arabella didn't mind, but this one felt special. It was so unusual.

She searched along the sideboard and Mark, as per usual, had left all his clutter out. It had become somewhat of a standing joke. Mark's books, bag, clothes, and jacket were strewn across a number of surfaces. He had a remarkable ability to shed stuff wherever he went. He also had the ability to never remember where he left all his belongings. She smiled as she fondly remembered the previous morning, when Mark left and returned to the house three times, each time coming back for something else. First his keys, then his wallet, and finally his jacket. Lily was in absolute stitches. Arabella picked up Mark's things, about to take them upstairs when something inside her suggested she look inside his bag.

She had never done this before. She wasn't even sure why she was doing it now. Of course her book wasn't going to be in there. She trusted Mark implicitly. I mean, they had just celebrated their seven-year wedding anniversary. Granted, she had given him a card and he hadn't given her anything but that's because he planned to take her away on a romantic weekend. Yes, she noticed Mark had been a little bit distant recently and was way too busy at work to bother with anything remotely Christmassy, but his behavior wasn't anything out of the ordinary. He always left her to do everything and Arabella as per usual had pulled out all the stops.

The girls had discussed their husbands at their last book club, competing with each other for the grand prize of which husband did the least.

Arabella had won.

She knew it sounded ridiculous to even think that her book could be in his bag but she needed a reason to peek inside. She felt uncomfortable! Her breath quickened and she looked around suspiciously. She felt guilty. Was she being watched? She sat for what seemed like forever staring at the bag. She could have sworn the bag was calling her name.

"Arabella open me! Your book is here. Come on, take a look. You know you want to."

What would her friends do? She imagined them sitting beside her. Alice would have dived into the bag long ago. Nicky might have thought about it first, then done it. Julie would probably say no but open it later in private. Jen would get everyone over with a bottle of wine and make an evening of it.

Arabella closed the blinds, locked the door and sat down, staring at the bag.

INDIANA JONES

Satipo: "Let us hurry, there is nothing to fear here."
Indiana: "That's what scares me."

Arabella sat there for what seemed like hours. She looked at the grandfather clock in the hall. Only thirty minutes had passed. It had begun to rain. Just a light pitter patter on the window. This reminded Arabella of book club the other night. They had been discussing this very situation. If you needed to, would you search your husband's things if you thought he was having an affair? Arabella had remembered her response. It hadn't involved much thought as it was an immediate "no" because why would she ever need to. Arabella and Mark were fine, no more problems than other couples, work got in the way and bills and money were always a contentious issue. She thought for a moment. They had been arguing slightly more over the last couple of months as he had been coming home later than usual after work. As long as it wasn't a repeat of last year, Arabella knew she could cope. Last year had been tough on both of them but they managed to put sticky plasters over it by talking it through with a professional.

"If you were to describe real happiness, what would that be?" the snooty counselor had asked Arabella at one of their sessions last year. Arabella didn't like the counselor at all. She was obviously in love with her husband Mark because anything Arabella said or did was entirely misconstrued. She was the second counselor they went to as Mark thought the first one fancied Arabella. How would this ever work if they couldn't even decide on marriage counselors? Oh, the irony. Most couples had problems though, it's how you dealt with the problems that made you stronger.

Another of the book club evenings had led the girls to discuss their ages. This year Arabella had hit thirty and everything changed. Her friends told her it would happen but she refused to believe them.

"It's hell, darling." Alice had said through a haze of cigarette smoke, knocking back a large double vodka.

"I bought a Porsche," Jen said.

"Whatever happens, we are here for you," Nicky said, clearly concerned. Julie gulped a sip of her large drink and remained silent.

"I feel great! You don't need to worry about me, I have everything I need," she said.

Arabella had planned her thirtieth meticulously as per usual. She had a spa morning with the girls, a bit of shopping with Lily in the afternoon and then a meal with Mark in the evening. But she woke up that birthday morning with the heaviest of hearts, as if the world had just come to an end.

Mark's thirtieth had been worse. The girls had invited the guys to their book club as a treat. The men sat outside talking manly stuff and the girls sat inside gossiping.

"He will be fine."

"I'm telling you darling, all it takes is for them to think they are too old or too fat and they run to the nearest available woman for reassurance."

"Just because your husband did it doesn't mean Mark will,

Alice."

"I'm just saying it's good to be aware."

"My Nick would never do anything like that, he knows he's too bald and fat to find anyone else. He bought a Porsche instead." Jen laughed.

"I'm just saying I think you need to be careful OK? You need to treat them like babies. Keep checking they're fed, watered, and happy at all times."

"Alice, give it a rest! Arabella doesn't want to hear this, not tonight."

Arabella sat quietly.

She would never need to know the signs.

They could make it through anything. She wasn't about to repeat their parents' behavior. No matter what, she would make it work, she wouldn't give up on them. Mark and she had agreed. If anyone felt the need to leave because they had met someone else, they would be honest and tell the other person straight away. Arabella trusted Mark. They would make it through as husband and wife whatever life was going to throw at them.

So here she was, at that 'sliding doors' moment.

Once Mark and Lily were finished shopping they were going ice skating which gave Arabella plenty of time to do whatever needed to be done.

Was Mark having an affair? Why this thought was entering her head now she wasn't sure. "It's okay Arabella, most women would want to know." She knew she was justifying her actions but she couldn't help herself. She didn't have much time, it was now or never. "Oh god, forgive me," she said as she grabbed Mark's bag.

It's not snooping. It's simply gathering information, she told herself. Even saying the word "snooping' filled her with dread.

Paranoid, she checked everything again: door locked–check, blinds down–check, car gone–check. She felt like Miss Moneypenny but not quite as attractive. She reached in the brown vintage leather bag she had bought for Mark when he got his first job. It had hidden pockets for his phone, keys and wallet. Arabella had no idea what she expected to actually find. Perhaps a piece of paper that read, "Yes I'm having an affair."

Instead, she found nothing. Nothing exciting anyway, apart from a couple of receipts and a few scribbled notes. She felt enormously relieved. This was not nearly as bad as she thought. Her mother's words entered her head "Every man will have an affair at one time or another, they can't help themselves." She wanted desperately to tidy his bag for him and sort the mess out but of course, she couldn't because then he would know she had been in it and that would make her a terrible spy.

Where else did Mark keep his things? Ah, yes, his desk! His desk was decorated simply, yet manly. A photo of the three of them and his notebook filled with ideas on all the businesses he was attempting to start, spruced up his desk. Mark was a serial entrepreneur. His normal job paid the bills but he was desperate to start his own business even though he was constantly coming up with ideas and never seeing them through. At one stage, he even expressed the desire to be prime minister. Arabella thought he was joking initially but when she realized he was being serious, no matter how unrealistic it seemed, she fully supported him. She had backed all his crazy ventures over the years and always hoped one of them would work out. She almost gave up her investigations when she discovered his laptop sitting in the corner begging to be opened. She knew it was always locked, but she tried to open it anyway. LOCKED! Next to it was Mark's iPad which she grabbed. It too was probably locked! She lifted it up, opened it, expecting to see the page that asked for the code. Instead it opened, and there was a photo of them all again. I mean, if he had been having an affair, he wouldn't parade his family around like this, would he? It was the picture they took from their last holiday in the South of France. Arabella smiled broadly. He obviously loved them a great deal. Why would he have that photo there if he didn't? She was so relieved! Of course he wasn't doing anything wrong. She hurriedly closed the iPad and put it back in its place. But a little voice spoke loudly in her head. That naughty voice that always got her into all sorts of trouble.

"If you don't look now, you won't get another opportunity, will you?"

The voice was right. This wasn't a time to be getting overtly sentimental. She was a spy on a mission. A mission that could save the world! Okay, maybe a step too far. What should she do? She looked around. Where was Cilla Black? "Surprise Surprise!" Maybe her friends were all going to jump out of the closet too, but no, nothing happened. Do it! Do it!

AMERICAN PIE

Finch: "God bless the internet"

Arabella snatched the iPad and ran into the loo with it. She slammed the door shut and reached to lock the door behind her. *Broken? Are you kidding me?* Unsurprisingly, Mark still hadn't fixed it.

Not being an international spy, she didn't know where exactly and in what folders she should start looking. She wasn't exactly appropriately dressed as a spy either. A black cat suit was what she needed, so she could stealthily make her way across the house. Like in *Oceans 11*. Or was it *12? Or 13?* She couldn't remember for the life of her. What she needed was a team, on the lookout as she completed her mission. She imagined the girls as an international spy group, and the book club was just their cover story. They were sent to help women sniff out their husbands' affairs.

What a great idea for a book, Arabella thought. She must remember to make a note of it.

Arabella calmed herself and put her detective hat on. Where to start… Social media. That was it! Okay, messages from anyone suspicious? No, only the usual drivel from Mark's ever-present fan club. That's what she had called the gaggle of girls who thought he was another Colin Firth. They should try living with him. That would certainly quell all their fantasies.

For Pete's sake Arabella, FOCUS. Arabella clicked on Mark's photos. There were a few pictures of Mark going out the other night. Arabella didn't recognize any of the names and continued to flick through the various pages.

OK, she thought, *let's try typing those names into the search bar and see what comes up.*

Lucy Anderson.......... Nothing.

Penelope Ellis........... Nothing.

"Oh this is pointless, what am I doing." Arabella squirmed on the toilet seat.

Betty Jones...

And there it was. Just like that.

There in black and white was an entire text message conversation that spanned the last three months.

"I miss you already."

"Last night was amazing."

"What the hell am I going to wear?"

"I will sort it."

"I woke up this morning, went downstairs and our song was playing on the radio."

"I wake up missing you a lot."

"You are my superhero."

And what's this...

Naked photos? No, no, no, no.

She sat there quickly scanning them all. Photos of them together, in a car, in a shop. Photos of shoes this woman was buying for Arabella's husband. Hotel rooms, photos of her on a boat, sipping a cocktail, looking sexy in underwear and bikinis. Why was this woman sending Arabella's husband photos of herself? Those boobs were not subtle either, there was no way Arabella could be misconstruing any of this.

Arabella felt numb. Her mother was right. Her friends were right. The world had in fact been right. He was having an affair. Her husband was having an affair and here was the proof. A bloody affair! Just saying the words sickened Arabella. Arabella heard Alice's voice going through the list of telltale signs your husband was having an affair. She was officially one of those foolish women who ignored them all. She hadn't checked that Mark was fed, watered and happy.

She was an utter idiot.

She wanted to believe Mark would never do this to her. And if not to her, at least not to Lily. If Arabella was being completely honest with herself though, she always had a niggling feeling that Mark would leave her. It all stemmed from the classic father syndrome. She knew being adopted and not knowing her father had caused many problems in her life she didn't quite want to face. She was a psychiatrist's dream. *"Marry someone like your father."*

OK Arabella, FOCUS. What should she do now? Her mother would tell her to breathe and not react in haste. She would also say, "I told you, darling, they all do it."

Arabella's mother was an exceptionally well off, very fashionable single lady who had decided after her fifth husband had died she would remain single. She was always asked out on dates but simply couldn't be bothered to go. She had a number of cats and quite frankly they were all she needed. She was highly intuitive though and only a few months previously had said to Arabella:

"Darling, watch that one. Something's not quite right."

Arabella had no control over her limbs. What do women do in this situation? Was there a helpline she could call? She couldn't speak. What she wanted to do was scream until the neighbours called 999 but not a sound came out of her mouth. She knew she had to act fast. What would these women tell her to do? They would tell her to find as much information out as she could and send it to herself as evidence. Oh God, where were her friends when she needed them? She sat there, fully ensconced in sending herself the photos and messages via email, knowing that she would read everything properly later when she'd had time to digest it all. She copied and pasted everything and hit SEND. Suddenly there was a knock on the door.

Crap!

Arabella jumped out of her skin, the iPad fell to the floor and she bumped her head on the boiler door. Maybe they would go away, Arabella hoped. Another knock, but this time louder, it thundered through the house. Arabella, shaken, crouched down to stop her knees from shaking. Did the police know she was there? Maybe they were watching her. Arabella held up the iPad and turned it around so she faced the camera. "Hello," she said eyeing the little circle. "Hellooooooo!" Nothing happened. A knock again halted Arabella's investigation. She had looked up at the bathroom window. If she tucked herself into a tiny ball, maybe she could fit. Why did she eat that piece of cake last night? Her bottom would most certainly get stuck and then she would have to be rescued by the fire brigade.

Mark would come home and find his iPad open on the toilet seat, he would know what she'd been up to. They would argue... Or, maybe a hot, hunky fireman would rescue her, they would fall madly in love and be ...

Knock! Knock!

Arabella remembered she was attempting to escape from prison. Okay, maybe not prison exactly, but it was stifling and she did feel trapped.

Arabella remained completely still. She didn't move a muscle. She waited... nothing. This must be the universe intervening again, telling her to hurry, she thought. She quickly found Betty's details and continued to email herself the photos, texts, everything. Now all she had to do was put the iPad back, but for some reason, Arabella couldn't move. Before she knew it, she clicked onto Betty's number and hit Facetime. What was she doing?

It rang and rang and rang. Arabella stared at the screen. Arabella realized she had absolutely no idea what she would say if Betty answered. She imagined herself in the movie *The Other Women*: the moment where after following your husband, you look across at him with another woman and have absolutely no idea what to do next. So you jump behind a bush only to land on a cactus.

"Betty, I'm Mark's wife!"

Granted, not the most original. She quickly pressed CANCEL. Thank goodness she didn't pick up!

Arabella returned everything she took with lightning speed. She ran back to the sitting room, opened the blinds, making sure nothing was out of place. So where should she stand when Mark walked in with Lily?

She walked into the kitchen and leaned against the table. No, that wasn't right! When would she ever do that? She ran back into the sitting room and sat flipping through a magazine, legs casually crossed. OK, this was getting ridiculous. She couldn't even remember the last time she read a magazine. Arabella gave up. She knew what she needed to do. She would look through all the dreaded information at Alice's house. She ran through a final check, making sure nothing was out of place before leaving the cottage. She looked back at the cottage as she locked the door. It didn't feel quite as homely as it had pre-discovery. A sinking feeling deep in the pit of her stomach threatened to derail her. Arabella stumbled down the lane, narrowly missing a parked car. *This is serious,* she thought.

As she walked down the lane, nothing looked quite so pretty anymore. The holly didn't look as red, the trees were droopier and there were no cute rabbits in her path. It was like the world already knew and it sensed her sadness. She kept on walking into the village, hoping she wasn't going to bump into anyone she knew. What would she say if she did? Arabella was in shock. This was like one of those films where the woman goes crazy and just starts running, like in *Forest Gump*. "Run, Forest, run." Arabella hated running though, so she could forget that ever happening. She couldn't run away from her problems, physically or metaphorically.

Arabella dropped her head, hoping to avoid eye contact with anyone she might see coming back from "The Village Panto" preparations. Because of her hospital appointment, she wasn't involved this year, thank goodness. She knew she should wait till she got to Alice's but she had to have another look! The emails were burning a hole inside her. What if she had got it wrong and had made a terrible mistake? Only one way to know for sure.

Arabella read and reread the messages as she walked. She really didn't want to look at the photos but knew she had to. There weren't many pictures of her face, only various parts of her body. Her young body. Her perfect body. No way had this woman given birth to a baby.

She surmised Betty and Mark had been seeing each other for a few months already. This was obvious from the dates on the messages. It also appeared from the messages that Betty was the perfect partner. They had gone out to several places in London to eat, "Bollinger" was mentioned several times as well as different restaurants Arabella had never heard of. She knew she was far from perfect; domestic goddess she was not. She tried making cakes once– the ones with all the frothy icing swirled as high as can possibly be, with all the special sprinkles – for Lily's last birthday. Let's just say, Lily and her friends declined her homemade treats and Arabella was forced to run to Tesco's to stock up. She tried painting, followed by card making, and finally gardening. All of which was a disaster, to say the least.

And then she tried writing.

Arabella loved writing! The words just poured out of her. This was going to be her year. The year where she could earn and treat Mark for a change. The year Mark would be proud of his wife. Or so she had thought until an hour ago.

Arabella imagined herself in court.

"Your Honour, I'd like to submit into evidence, the people's exhibit 4. This clearly shows my husband cavorting with another woman."

"I'd like to take a closer look please, just to check these are in fact Mrs. Jones' bits."

Bloody hell, even the judge would probably find her attractive. Betty was on a boat in two of the photos. Was that Barbados? Hold on, that was Mark's wash bag in that photo in a very expensive looking bathroom. Arabella couldn't take it anymore.

"I think you deserve more, that's all," she had written him. "I would give everything up to be with you at Christmas."

What was that? This woman wanted to spend Christmas with Mark?

"Happy two months!" Arabella quickly worked out this meant they had been seeing each other since October. She immediately shut her phone down. She didn't deserve this. No-one deserves this!

And especially not at Christmas.

She needed a drink. She hardly ever drank but a large vodka sounded perfectly good right now. Arabella had already passed all the local pubs in the village so she would have to make do with a chai tea at her favourite coffee shop before climbing the hill to Alice's. She walked into "Granny's" and the kind "Hello" that greeted her made her want to burst into tears and tell them everything that just happened. She kept her composure however and ordered a drink. She then ducked into the toilet and grabbed a handful of tissues.

Arabella looked at her pathetic self in the mirror and sobbed.

She cried for what she had lost and she cried for what she was about to lose. She honestly believed that she and Mark could get through anything and now her entire future was in jeopardy. As she looked down at her feet and then to her hands and finally back to her face again she saw herself as Julia Roberts in *Erin Brockovich*. Not the part where she was going to save the world but the bit before, where she was a penniless mother. Where would Lily and Arabella live? How would they survive? She had devoted her life to being a mother and wife. Yes, the house was in both Mark and Arabella's names but she had no finances of her own. She heard her mother's voice saying, "It's all about the execution darling." Well yes, that was an option. She could execute him, although she didn't think that's what she had meant.

Arabella knew what she did now was of utmost importance. She needed to be smart and plan her next steps very carefully. Alice would know what to do, she had been divorced once before and her current husband had recently dallied on the dark side.

As Arabella raced up the hill, she realized she hadn't brought a coat and it was freezing. Had she even locked the door? Oh well, if the house got robbed at least it would all be Mark's stuff that got stolen. She began tracing her movements as she left the house when she bumped into Lily's teacher, Mrs. Taz.

"Hello Arabella."

"Oh, hi."

"How are the preparations going for the village panto?" Mrs. Taz asked Arabella.

Arabella could act normal, couldn't she? Yes, everything was perfectly fine. No-one knew what she knew. She was still Lily's mum and she was still Mark's wife and no-one knew a thing. If she didn't tell anyone, then it wouldn't be real. She could keep it to herself and it would all go away.

"All good I think," was all she could manage. Followed by, "Sorry I have to go, I have an appointment."

"Okay, well, let me know if there is anything I can help with. Will Mark be at the Panto too?"

Mrs. Taz's question stopped Arabella in her tracks. Was Mrs. Taz having an affair with Mark too? Maybe he had slept with everyone in the neighborhood and Arabella was the laughing stock of the village.

"I damn well hope not, because I'll kill him and bury him in the vegetable patch."

"No, I don't think so. We have family stuff on that day," she managed to answer with a smile. She thought she saw a flash of disappointment in Mrs. Taz's eyes but she recovered quickly.

"Happy Christmas and see you tomorrow then." Mrs. Taz waved her on.

****

Arabella was exhausted when she arrived at Alice's studio and dreaded sharing the latest events. She also knew the minute she actually said the words, "affair" and "Mark" in the same sentence, then there was no going back. Her world would come crashing down around her. As it turned out, she didn't have to say anything. Arabella's face as she locked eyes on Alice painted an extremely vivid picture.

Alice quickly shut up her studio, "Costumes can wait, come on upstairs."

Alice's studio, a gorgeous design shop with costumes from all around the world that she had collected on her travels, was a favorite place of Arabella's. Alice was incredibly talented, her talents wasted working on only local projects. Each wall was covered with memorabilia, bits of fabric or things that "could one day be used," which was Alice's favourite saying.

The space sat empty for ages available for rent as it was too small for a normal shop and too big for an office. But as a little studio and consultation area, it worked brilliantly. A year later and Alice had no intention to leave.

Arabella, white and shell shocked, sat down.

"Tell Aunty Alice what's wrong."

Arabella tried to speak but stopped herself.

"I can guess honey. C'mon, tell me what's going on."

Arabella was afraid if she started to share the awful story she might implode.

"You were right," was all she could manage to say.

"You need a drink."

Alice reached into a glass cabinet and lifted a top hat. There, underneath it were two glasses. She lifted a witch's hat next to it and there was a bottle of gin.

"For emergencies," she said.

Arabella started to fill Alice in. How she had listened to the universe just like she had told her to and proceeded to uncover the scandal.

Arabella opened her emails and showed Alice the forwarded messages and photos.

Alice's jaw dropped.

"Oh my god, I don't want to say I told you so, but…"

"I know."

"She must have had a boob job, they are not real. Look at that boat! You can clearly see her face is entirely botoxed. I'm surprised she can even open her mouth. What is she drinking, is that a margarita?"

Arabella stared at Alice blankly.

"Yes sorry, back to the point. I can't believe it, Mark of all people!"

"Look, it mentions "things we have done". There are photos of them shopping for Christmas presents. Look at the dates, look at them! LOOK!"

"It even mentions my name," Arabella said, pointing to one that said, *"I hope Arabella doesn't see the post it notes on the presents, I was worried you would leave one on and she would see it."*

"They went shopping together, they've bought Lily's Christmas present, a mug!"

Alice continued to read, "Seems like more of a pornographic novel if you ask me."

"They even talk about their future honeymoon to Bora Bora."

Arabella could hardly speak in between her sobs.

"They want to move to America and set up a business! Another bloody idea of Mark's I'm sure."

"SOULMATE, FUCKING SOULMATES!"

Alice knew it was bad, Arabella never swore.

"What are you going to do now?" Alice asked.

"I'm not sure. Mark and Lily are still out and we have Christmas planned here. How can I possibly sit at home knowing all of this?"

"I don't know, I really don't. But you have to take care of Lily and you have to take care of yourself. Have you told anyone else?"

"No-one, only you."

"Good, don't."

"What do you mean?"

"You are going to pretend you know nothing."

"Have you lost your mind? How can I possibly do that?"

"You have no other choice, Arabella. You need to think about Lily."

"Yes, but how on earth am I going to manage that? I feel like I've been punched in the stomach a zillion times. I have been lied to for months."

"Arabella, you can do this! I know this isn't what you want to hear, but you need to do this for Lily's sake. You have to think very carefully before you make any rash decisions. Believe me, you will thank me after."

"Are you sure?"

"Your future is at stake here Arabella. It won't be easy, but I'm here for you whenever you need me. Do you want me to tell the girls for you?"

"No, I think I'll wait. I need to sort my head out first. You're right, it only just happened." Arabella wiped her tears with a shaky hand.

"I need to call my mother."

She mustered a small amount of inner strength, left Alice's studio and headed home. She could do this. Alice was right, Lily was all that mattered and her daughter meant everything to her. She thought back to when Lily crawled for the first time, said her first word and started the first day of school. Arabella pulled herself together. She would do this for Lily.

INDECENT PROPOSAL

Diana: "If you ever want something badly, let it go. If it comes back to you then it's yours forever, if it doesn't then it was never yours to begin with."

Arabella walked aimlessly along the cobbled streets, lightheaded, feeling sick, happy families looking back at her. Their family too was supposed to be enjoying the festivities. Tears threatened to start all over again but Arabella caught herself.

"Right, pull yourself together! This is your family, dammit. Now fight for it! You have to focus on Lily."

Arabella opened her front door and immediately things felt different. The homely feeling she worked tirelessly to create was now gone. She saw everything in a different light. Mark's jacket loomed out of place amongst their things and the photos on the walls didn't seem quite so happy. It was as if she was now living in a Salvador Dali painting where reality was there but nothing made sense.

She plugged her phone in as it was nearly dead and poured herself a glass of ice cold water. There was no point putting it off any longer, she needed to do it now. Arabella dialed her mother's number. It rang and went straight to answerphone.

"You've clearly called at an inconvenient time. I'm out doing something important with highly influential people but if you leave a message I will return your call."

"Hi Mummy, it's me. I've got something to tell you. Anyway, plans over Christmas might be different so call me when you can. Love you."

She very rarely said "I love you," but today Arabella couldn't stop herself.

What was she to do now? The plans she envisioned for the year seemed totally irrelevant. Her marriage was what was important now.

If there was still a marriage, of course.

Lists always helped Arabella in times like these. Yes, she needed to make a list. Scrummaging around, she found her writing book in a drawer. If only she had looked there first! And yet, then she would have just gone on not knowing. Which was worse?

She leaned back on the sofa, gazing up at the ceiling, gathering her thoughts. Mark and Lily would be back soon. She needed a game plan and she needed it quickly. Mark texted her on the way back to the house.

"Lily is hungry and we've done enough shopping for the year." Why he couldn't just buy her something to eat, she wasn't sure. Were there no cafes or restaurants in London? Maybe he couldn't take Lily to them because he had already been to them with Betty. This overthinking was going to kill her. She kept seeing the messages in her head. "8i8" What the heck that meant, she had no idea. Mark and Betty had said it to each other a lot, as well as celebrating their week by week anniversaries like two high-schoolers. How cruel was Mark? She started writing in her book:

What should I do? Not an inventive title, but it did the job.

1) *Try and win Mark back.*

They were meant to be together forever, that's what marriage meant, right? What if he didn't want her back though? Then what? She thought about *The Twits* by Roald Dahl and recalled the tricks they played on each other. She could at least make him suffer for having an affair.

2) *Forget about Mark.*

Turns out it was going to be a very short list.

They had planned to go away as a family after Christmas to celebrate the New Year. Arabella wondered if moving the trip forward was a better option. If Mark was intending to see this other woman at Christmas, then she had to try to prevent that. She wanted to give Mark and Lily a Christmas to remember.

And suddenly it was decided. Arabella would save her marriage. Her life depended on it.

She dialed Mark's phone. Lily picked up.

"Hello my darling, are you still with Daddy?"

"Yes, just heading home. Why?"

She loved it when Lily used grown up expressions.

"Well Mummy has an idea. How about you pick up a few extra things for us? I will text Daddy the list."

Arabella hung up, proceeded to write a huge list and texted it to Mark.

Santa outfit, Mrs Claus outfit, more food, candles, tree, lights, more presents, the list went on. She could see Mark's face now. He was so incredibly tight with money and now she realized why. He was keeping another woman. She couldn't forget the photos and receipts for flowers and gifts she definitely hadn't received and evenings out she definitely hadn't been on. Seems like they had been out with "mutual" friends and even the family had met her.

Arabella suddenly threw caution to the wind and decided to live dangerously. Bugger her damn list. This was a time for drastic measures! She would book them a cabin. A cabin in a pretty French resort where they would be isolated from reality. Mark would not be able to refuse. He loved skiing and had been promising for years to take Lily when she was old enough. Arabella secretly hated the snow, but this was the perfect idea.

Arabella wondered why they had never gone away before for Christmas? She envisioned them on a snowcapped mountain, laughing and hugging. Drinking hot chocolate together in front of a roaring log fire. Mark would tell her he loved her and that she was the only woman for him. They would sledge down with huskies, pull up to the Christmas lit cabin and have a magical meal.

Arabella ran upstairs and opened the loft where the cases were kept. They were very dusty as they hadn't been used for some time. She reached for Mark's case and noticed it wasn't quite as dirty as the others. In fact, it had a tag on that she hadn't written. She ran back downstairs, grabbed her phone and looked back at the forwarded messages and photos from Mark's phone. That bathroom with the wash bag... that was a hotel room! Her face sank.

He had been away, WITH HER.

Arabella, crestfallen, wondered why she was bothering at all. There was no way she could see this through. She plodded back upstairs and sat amongst the cases. She looked across the hallway into Lily's room. Lily. This Christmas was for Lily, remember? She picked up the bags, threw them on her bed and began packing like a woman possessed. Decorations, presents, clothes, they all went in. She stopped. Oh crap! She hadn't actually found a cabin. You see, this is why she wrote things down, this is why she planned.

Back downstairs she opened her laptop and typed in "Christmas cabins in France." Nothing except very expensive private homes to buy. She tried again. "Christmas cabins for short stay." Bingo! As she scrolled down the page they got cheaper and cheaper until she saw "Cancellations." Perfect!

She found a cute little cabin and before she knew what she was doing, she booked it. She looked up to the sky, "Thank you universe," she mouthed. She had gone and done it. Phase one of the plan, completed. She felt a small sense of accomplishment. All Mark and Lily had to do was turn up.

Mark and Lily were taking much longer that Arabella had anticipated. The list was obviously proving to be quite a feat. Arabella wandered around the cottage, soaking everything in. She knew once they returned from their holiday, things would be different. She thought about Mark's family. Had they known about Betty all this time? Arabella had so many unanswered questions swirling through her head, she needed some way to release her anxiety about it all.

As she grabbed her notebook and a pretty Tiffany pen, Arabella noticed her wedding ring. She twirled it slowly around her finger, remembering the day had Mark proposed. She couldn't remember feeling any happier than that moment. She was the luckiest girl in the world. But it didn't mean anything, did it? It was just reminding her of all of Mark's lies and deceit.

Was she supposed to remove her wedding ring?

Thinking about it, Arabella couldn't remember seeing Mark wearing his ring for a while. He told her he was having it cleaned, and then said he hadn't picked it up. How was she ever going to believe anything he said ever again? He had been lying to her for months.

Arabella, you can do this, you have to stay strong!

As she continued writing down her thoughts, she saw the lights of Mark's car pull into the driveway. Arabella stood up, pen and paper in hand and looked at herself in the mirror. "Most important acting job of your life. Let's do this!" She plastered on a fake smile and opened the door. Mark marched into the house laden with bags, followed by a tearful Lily who was carrying nothing.

"What happened?"

"Lily wanted a costume and I said no."

"Why, how much was it?"

"That's not the point."

"Well, what is the point then? It's Christmas."

"We have enough already. You spoil her."

This was enough to make Arabella's blood boil, but instead of reacting she immediately sat down and began writing in her notebook. Yes, this writing thing would be her lifeline and save her. Literally.

Mark stared at her and mumbled angrily, "What on earth are you doing?"

"I just remembered a few things I forgot on my list."

Turns out, lying to Mark was surprisingly easy. Is that how he felt when he lied to her for all those months?

Arabella and Mark never agreed on money, ever. They both had very different values as far as money was concerned. Arabella believed when you had only one child you spoiled them, especially at Christmas. Mark vehemently disagreed. Arabella tried to buy presents throughout the year to save money but there were always last-minute extras. Arabella did the same for birthdays. Every birthday Arabella experienced the same thing...

"I can't believe you haven't done anything for my birthday," Arabella stared blankly at Mark that last fall. "I don't ask for much. All I wanted was something that you and Lily made together. I always think about you when it's your birthday. Was it a surprise this year, was the day sprung upon you?"

Mark, embarrassed, knew Arabella was right. Even if things were off between them, this wasn't fair.

"I don't know what to say."

"You're never here, Mark! You make no effort at all." Although Mark realized this was partly true, he also believed he showed his love for his family by going to work.

"I just hadn't thought about it like that. You and Lily are always on my mind."

"I know, I'm sorry."

"I'm working to take care of us. You two mean the world to me."

Arabella's tone softened. "But it isn't just about the money,

Mark."

She knew money was what most couples argued about and they had the same argument over and over again. She grew up in a family that argued about the lack of money constantly.

Now, standing here in the house, knowing what she knew, Arabella was determined to save the day. She picked Lily up, comforting her. She was still upset and Mark looked thoroughly pissed off. Well, this seemed as good a time as any to tell them about their trip.

"Look, whilst you were out Mummy planned something very special."

Lily stopped sulking and watched Arabella with great interest.

"We're going away! We leave tomorrow. To a cabin! SURPRISE! You always said you wanted snow at Christmas."

Arabella beamed.

Lily was thrilled.

Mark looked like he'd been run over by a freight train.

TEN THINGS I HATE ABOUT YOU

Bianca: "Has the fact that you're a complete psycho managed to escape your attention?"

Mark was so tired from his escapades with Lily, he had no energy to question or argue over Arabella's bomb shell. He fell asleep early that night, knowing their trip was a foregone conclusion. Arabella lay there for hours, reading and re-reading the messages and seeing the photos on her email, feeling lonelier than she had ever felt before. There were small moments of pleasure when she read an argument Mark and Betty had had, or when he had not bought her the Christmas present she obviously wanted. She woke up at the crack of dawn to finish packing and prepare all the shopping, distracting herself from the misery that threatened to engulf her at any moment. This was the most important Christmas of their lives.

Everything needed to be perfect.

They left the cottage early, the village barely awake. Lily sang to herself in the back of the car as Mark drove quietly, seemingly happy enough. Maybe she had imagined the affair, everything seemed so normal. If she closed her eyes and opened them, perhaps she would realize the last twenty-four hours was all a dream. They were a family and they were still happy. She rested her eyes before they hit the chunnel. She told Lily that they would have to hold their breath when they went under the water and if they were lucky, they might see mermaids and Nemo.

So far, the journey was plain sailing. They stopped a couple of times, to go to the loo and fill the car up with petrol. Once through the other side they made their way down through France. The roads were surprisingly empty as people must have departed early for their destinations hoping to miss traffic. They headed towards the mountains; the blue sky appeared, leaving the grey skies behind them.

Arabella couldn't help thinking about the messages and images she had seen on Mark's iPad. She pondered over them repeatedly as they drove towards the cabin, stressing herself out in the process.

Focus, Arabella, focus!

If the next few days were to work out then she couldn't lose track. She thought back to her list. Did she even want him back now? Perhaps some fun would keep her from losing her mind completely. She started plotting. She took out her new notebook and pen and began writing again. Her notebook had been a gift from Julie and was a lovely gesture. Julie was the quieter one of the group. She wasn't flashy and would do thoughtful things, always under the radar. Arabella had mentioned to the girls weeks before that she was thinking of writing. One morning when Arabella went downstairs to empty the bins, she opened the front door and sitting on the porch was a little gift addressed to her. The card read:

"For your special words."

It was such a pretty little book. A bright yellow book that said "Keep your happy."

"What are you doing?" Mark asked inquisitively.

"Just writing. Someone mentioned the other day they liked my stories and suggested I write them down. So I thought I would give it a go."

Mark guffawed.

"You? Words? Really?"

He was mocking her. The treacherous liar was mocking her!

Day one: Mark is a gigantic arse! Okay, it wasn't Keats but she'd get there.

Arabella desperately wanted the fun to start. Mark was driving along seemingly without a care in the world and Lily was still singing to herself. How could she possibly sing the same song non-stop for seven whole hours? She loved her daughter dearly but if something didn't change, Arabella might throw herself out of the moving car.

Mark really had no idea what Arabella was going through. She felt nauseous at the thought of keeping up this charade for the next few days. Until now, her life had been organized. In the space of one day, it had been reduced to a mass of uncertainty. Her sleepless night obsessing over all the emails, of course, didn't help matters, and even though she felt shattered, something almost robotic took over her body. This must be what they call survival, Arabella mused.

She remembered in one of the messages, Betty had referred to a song that was now "their' song. They had a song together? Great! Arabella felt particularly masochistic at this point and wondered how Mark would react if she pushed him slightly. She logged onto her iTunes and downloaded "their song." It didn't matter that she had to download the whole album. It would be worth it to see him squirm as he listened to the music. Would he have fond memories of the concert he and Betty had gone to?

"How long now?" Arabella asked.

"Not much further. We should get there just before dark." Mark replied.

"Thank you for driving. I don't know why I'm so tired today."

"I don't mind, although my back is starting to ache a little bit and I need to pull in for some water."

"But I packed plenty," Arabella answered innocently. There was a large pause. She knew exactly what Mark was thinking. *You want to speak to your trollop, don't you?*

"I need to speak to my brother before it's too late," he said.

"Ok, let me call him for you."

Arabella searched through her phone for his number.

"Ummm no that's okay it's about work!" Mark answered far too quickly. "I can pull in here and just call him."

"Honestly my darling, it's no trouble." Arabella countered.

Did he think she was a complete idiot? How many excuses was he going to make in order to stop the car to secretly call Betty? Was this how it was going to be the entire holiday? Arabella looked at Mark, waiting for his next move.

Silence.

"I actually need to use the loo anyway so let's pull over and sort ourselves out."

He was stupid and cruel.

As they pulled into the petrol station, Arabella turned to Lily. She had to think quickly. "Lily my darling, go in with Daddy and get some treats for the car, would you?"

She knew Lily wouldn't be able to say no to that and Mark would have no choice but to watch Lily. Project Mark vs Arabella had begun. Granted, it wasn't the most original name but she was still new at this writing thing.

She opened her book and wrote. *Mark 0, Arabella 1.*

Mark got out and walked across the forecourt with Lily skipping behind him. She could have sworn she saw him looking at her with daggers. She turned back to her phone. Great, the tune had downloaded. Now she had to make sure it played when he got back. On repeat!

As Mark restarted the car, he flipped through his messages. Arabella knew it wasn't work. It was Christmas Eve for goodness sake. She innocently turned to Mark.

"Can we not be on our phones all through Christmas? It would be lovely if we could focus on the three of us."

She massaged Mark's neck and ran her fingers through his hair. He flinched slightly at her touch, a sharp pain hitting Arabella directly in her gut. He didn't want her! She was going to throw up.

Arabella had to do something to distract herself.

"Wouldn't it be lovely if Mummy and Daddy weren't on their phones this week my darling?"

She implored Lily to agree but Lily was wrapped up in her own world, talking to herself. A world Arabella would currently quite like to join.

Arabella turned back to Mark, "Yep, Lily agrees."

Mark was so obviously lost in his own world thinking of Betty and clearly just wanted to get to their destination so he could call her.

"Didn't everyone at the Panto feel like you were abandoning them?" Mark said.

"No, I was supposed to be recovering, remember?"

Silence.

"What made you decide to book this then?"

Arabella wondered why Mark was suddenly asking all these questions. She was ready though. She refused to get caught off guard and had plotted briefly with Alice via text late last night.

"Well, it just made me think that maybe I was given a chance to really enjoy Christmas. You know, by not being in hospital. I wanted to make the most of us all being together," Arabella answered sweetly.

Mark smiled and didn't say anything more on the subject. It was hard knowing she would miss out on the village panto. They had been part of it every year since they moved to the village and she always helped out backstage. Arabella hoped one year Lily might actually want to be in it. This year would have ruined all those lovely memories, though. The last thing she wanted was a re-enactment of *Love Actually*, where Emma Thompson finds out her husband is having an affair and on the evening of the panto tells her husband, Alan. The entire scene was heart-wrenching to watch. Arabella had watched the movie a hundred times and always fast forwarded that section.

How ironic, she currently found herself in the exact same position.

Arabella looked at Mark. He did seem different and a little distant for sure. She tried again to touch him, putting her hand on his leg as he drove. She tried to remember when they had last made love but for the life of her, she couldn't think of it. It couldn't have been that long ago, surely? Eight weeks? She had been so preoccupied preparing for Christmas, she had totally forgotten.

They had regularly discussed their love life or lack of it at "Book Club." Alice and her hubby were at it like rabbits most of the time but the others were rather sporadic at best, depending on who they had to babysit and what they had on at the weekend. They were lucky if they could lie in for a few hours at the weekend. When you have kids, everything changes. No-one tells you that part when you go to prenatal classes and no-one provides guidance through those difficult, formative years. *Now that would be a good business to start up,* Arabella thought. Marriage counseling before you actually needed it. A self-help group for couples on the start of their journey together, rather than at the end of it.

She suddenly remembered she had surprised Mark with a romantic night only a couple of months ago. This must have been overlapping when he first met Betty. Lily was safely at her grandmother's and Arabella went all out. She lit candles and made a meal from scratch. Okay, she had one delivered, but she unpacked it all on her own.

Mark was surprised but also seemed really pleased. She met him at the door wearing only a fur coat, suspenders and high heels. Mark loved suspenders. She waited in anticipation, unsure of his reaction. But he threw down his briefcase, picked her up and carried her to their bedroom where they had a wonderful evening. After they had made love, they spoke about how they were really going to try and think of each other during the day and make each other feel special when they spent any time together. Mark looked into her eyes and told her he loved her.

Arabella was perplexed. There had been good times, she wasn't imagining this! Arabella re-read the text messages that he had sent her that night to make sure she wasn't going crazy.

"Thank you for last night. I love you!"

Arabella turned to Mark and spoke quietly. "I know it was a little while ago, but do you remember the other night? Maybe we can do that again. What do you say?"

"Did you bring the fur?"

She nodded flirtatiously and pressed play on the stereo for maximum effect. The words from "their song." blared through the speakers.

"Oh, I love this song! This should be our holiday song, don't you think?" Arabella watched Mark closely for any signs of guilt. "Lily, you love this song, don't you?"

Lily, surprised, had no idea what her mother was talking about. She had never heard this song and she really couldn't care less about it.

"Let's make this our holiday song. Sing Lily, sing!" Arabella shrilled like a mad woman. She knew she was behaving like a lunatic but Mark was acting like everything was normal. Rage building on the inside of her, Arabella couldn't tear her gaze from Mark. Wow, not even a wince. How could he be so calm and collected? He must know, surely? How could he not? Or was he deliberately being obtuse? Bugger! Now she would have to listen to this awful song all bloody holiday.

"Two hours till we get there," he muttered.

Arabella began singing at the top of her lungs. She needed to do something to mask the self-doubt about to choke her even if she did sound like an overzealous Cockatoo.

Maybe this wasn't such a sensible idea. Maybe she should just tell him now that she knows about Betty and end this charade. She leaned over and nuzzled his throat. She bit hard into his neck, blood oozing from his jugular vein. He swerved and lost control of the car, crashing into a tree. Arabella, bloodied and bruised reached for Lily. "Lily! Baby?" Arabella, dizzy, dragged herself out of the car and around to Lily's side. She was alive, but Mark wasn't breathing. Arabella checked for a pulse, but nothing. He must have died on impact. Arabella had no time to grieve. She had to get Lily out of there, to safety. As soon as she pulled Lily away from the mangled wreck and over to the side of the road, the car burst into flames. Lily screamed, desperate to save her father but it was too late. They watched as the paramedics removed Mark's burnt body from the wreckage.

"Arabella. Arabella?"

Was that Lily?

"Arabella wake up!" Arabella jumped. She saw Lily smiling down at her. She must have dozed off for a second. Of course she didn't want Mark to die.

Well not yet anyway.

Think nice thoughts, Arabella. Nice thoughts. Maybe just a slight skiing accident or a broken finger? A pulled groin muscle would be perfect, actually.

"Yes, Lily."

"Mummy, what's the plan when we get to our cabin? I'm a bit tired."

Arabella hadn't given much thought to what might happen once they arrived at the cabin. What exactly were her choices? A broken family? Or a dead husband? Well she did love Mark and she adored their little family, so she had to stay strong. This other woman was not going to destroy what they had built together. Yes, she vacillated between killing him and handing him over to Betty but for now, she would not give up.

"Mummy has lots planned, my darling."

Right now Arabella's only plan was to make Mark realize he was making the biggest mistake of his life. Alice, never short of advice, encouraged her to do so.

"Make small changes so he feels disorganized and realizes he can't live without you. At the same time, make this a perfect family Christmas," she said.

Arabella thought about her friends manically getting ready for the panto and her cozy house all lonely without its Christmas lights. Mrs. Deary had promised she would "keep an eye on things" whilst they were away.

"You never know what might happen at Christmas time with burglaries, deary."

As they arrived in the little French mountain village, the snow started to fall. It was so beautiful Arabella felt an ache in her chest. How she wished they had come here under different circumstances. She could make a beautiful photo album from their trip and show it to their grandchildren. Did they still have a chance? Arabella wanted to believe it so badly.

"I think it's this way. Second on the left apparently."

Arabella directed Mark down a little street and up a driveway. Everything was pitch black.

"I hope the lights work when we get there," Mark quipped.

"Don't worry, I brought candles and a torch," Arabella said.

"You're amazing, you know that?" Mark grinned at Arabella, seemingly genuine.

There it was, a glimmer of hope. They still had something. They still had something worth fighting for. Arabella was secretly elated.

Once Mark parked beside the cabin, he pulled out his phone and jumped out of the car.

"Quick, chase him!" Arabella yelled at Lily.

"What?" Lily answered, confused.

"Get your shoes on darling. Hurry! "It's a Christmas game called 'Don't leave daddy's side,' OK?"

Lily, completely flummoxed, did as she was told.

Arabella was forced to improvise. Lily didn't know the rules of the game but immediately did as she was told. She loved to play and also knew there would be chocolate at the end of it. She leapt out of the car and chased her father. Mark quickly put his phone away as Lily grabbed his hand. He looked down at her with such love Arabella thought her heart would break in two. She must not cry! If she started now she wouldn't stop and she had a plan to set in motion.

She unpacked the car and carried their belongings inside. The cabin was adorable! From the little she could see, it had a spectacular view of the mountains. A real fireplace sat in a corner, accompanied by a large open plan living area. She wanted it to feel like their home away from home. Whatever happened this Christmas, Arabella wanted Lily to have fond memories of their time here.

Lily ran back in with Mark, after a little exploring. "Mummy, can I see my bedroom?"

"Of course darling, go ahead!"

****

Arabella tried to ignore it when Mark excused himself to go and get firewood for the tenth time and came back with nothing. Did she really have "fool" tattooed on her forehead? As she went upstairs, she looked out of the window and saw Mark's phone light up. He must be messaging her!

Be strong, Arabella. You cannot allow this woman to destroy your marriage. Mark would never give everything up for someone he had just met.

Arabella almost believed herself.

Where the hell is my notebook? she thought.

Mark walked in with a renewed spring in his step. "I thought I would go and get you a Starbucks my darling."

"Are you sure? Isn't it a bit late?" Arabella asked knowing full well that Mark wanted to call Betty in secret again.

"I just looked on Google, it's open twenty-four hours. You've worked so hard this Christmas. I just want to do something nice for my wife." Mark smiled sexily, clearly hoping to distract her. The cheek of the man never ceased to surprise her. He had no idea who he was up against.

"Lily do you want to go with Daddy?" Arabella quickly interjected.

"Oh it's too late for Lily, she should be going to bed." Mark hastily added.

"Why, it's Christmas Eve?" Arabella smirked.

Lily hopped up and down with glee.

"Lily, shoes on, off you go!" Arabella practically pushed Lily out of the door towards the car.

Mark glowered at her. She smiled back, sweetly feigning ignorance. *You're going to have to be a little smarter, my dear husband, if you intend to get past me this holiday.*

Lily, completely unaware of any tension, turned to Arabella and whispered. "Are we still playing the game mummy?"

"Yes my darling, it's a long game that's going to last all Christmas."

Lily, delighted, bounded after her father.

Arabella watched as the car pulled out of the driveway.

Arabella had to think quickly. This might be the only time she would have to herself. She opened up Mark's case, not sure what she was going to find. *No, Arabella, Betty is not tucked away in there.* Arabella was losing it, that's for sure.

Nothing popped out except for Mark's charger. Arabella

considered this. If his phone wasn't charged then he wouldn't be able to speak to Betty, now would he? She carefully picked up the charger and attempted to hide it. The wardrobe? No, way too obvious. Lily's room? Nah, that would be the second place he would look. Arabella spotted an old-fashioned cushion with a zip. PERFECT. Mark was so preoccupied, he wouldn't even notice his charger was missing for a few hours anyway.

She smiled to herself and went downstairs. Only three days to go. She could do it. Now time to make the place look spectacular. A fake Christmas tree with bright lights stood proudly in the corner. Lily and Mark could add the decorations later. Arabella packed the food in the fridge and arranged the presents under the tree. Presents without "post it notes on" from Betty. Nearly done. Now for the beautiful mantelpiece. She hung up their stockings, all three of them, with their perfectly stitched initials on each one.

Mark entered the house with Starbucks and Lily in tow. He looked like the old Mark returning to his family. He even kissed Arabella as he handed her the treat. Arabella had this awful feeling again that she had misread everything. She ran upstairs and once again re-read the messages from Betty to Mark on her phone. No, no mistake here.

"I miss you, I love you, let's go away. Can't wait for you to come home. Two weeks is too long. I can't wait to have you inside me again...."

Unless she had completely lost her mind, these were not messages that you received from a friend. Aware Lily might pop in on her, she took her phone into the bathroom. She read the messages about the private things Mark and Betty had done together. Bile rose up suddenly, lodging in Arabella's throat. This couldn't be happening. She bent over the toilet, afraid she might throw up. Arabella remembered how Mark loved it when she caressed him and rubbed his tummy. She thought about all the intimate moments they had shared together that were now moments he was sharing with another woman. Was it because she had said no to certain things? Was Betty sexually more adventurous? It seemed it was true from these messages. You try being a mother Betty! You'd be lucky to fit in a quick one before you were summoned to help your child with something.

How could he do this? They'd had a pact! They had promised each other that if either of them wanted to end their marriage for whatever reason, they would be up front and honest about it. Especially if it involved someone else. But Mark was now not only having an affair, he was lying to her about it. He was willingly deceiving her and that made Arabella hopping mad. Mark was going to get exactly what he deserved.

Arabella wiped away her tears, pulled herself together, and went back downstairs to join them. She watched the two loves of her life decorating the tree.

The perfect family portrait.

It could have been if she hadn't known the grisly truth about the affair. This was how she imagined Christmas as a family. She picked up her phone and began snapping photos of the three of them, needing to capture these memories, knowing this could be their last family Christmas together. As Mark got out the presents and placed them under the tree, Arabella remembered the message she had seen from Betty.

I bought Lily a Little Miss Sunshine cup, I hope she likes it.

Arabella tried to remain calm but anger rose up inside her. How could Mark have gone Christmas shopping with Betty? Interesting how he had time for a romantic shopping spree when he managed to convince Arabella that work afforded him no opportunity to do so. Unanswered questions bred more unanswered questions and before she knew it, Arabella couldn't stop the mayhem erupting in her mind. Did he take Betty for a little candlelit meal after shopping? Or had it been a quick rendezvous in the middle of Mark's work day? Arabella used to go and see Mark in the day, but real life had taken over. She thought she saw a glimmer of a smile as he put the presents out. Was he remembering their Christmas shopping trip to Selfridges?

"The cabin looks wonderful." Mark's voice brought her back down to earth with a mighty thud. Yes, it did look beautiful and she felt quite proud of herself, especially under the circumstances.

"Lily, would you like to place the fairy on the top of the tree?" Arabella asked her daughter.

This was a family ritual that started when Lily was a toddler. They waited for Mark, even if he had been at work all day, so they could put the final touches on the tree. Brimming with excitement, Lily jumped into Mark's arms and he lifted and held her there as she put the fairy on top. She couldn't imagine what Christmas would be like next year. Who would place the fairy on the tree?

She envisioned herself and Lily on the street as they peered inside a mansion house. They could see people laughing and having fun, standing alongside the biggest Christmas tree you've ever seen. As Arabella and Lily, dressed in rags, ran to the front door begging for scraps, the door suddenly opened. Standing at the door were Mark and Betty, dripping in jewels and laden with gifts.

"Go away, you're not wanted here," said Betty, eyeing them with disgust.

"Oh please Mark, don't forget us, please!"

"I don't know who these beggars are Betty, get rid of them," Mark snapped.

Arabella was jogged back to reality by Lily's giggles. Arabella watched Mark playing with Lily by the tree. No, he would never forget them.

Would he?

SLIDING DOORS

Helen: "For god's sake Gerry, I asked you a simple question. There's no need for you to become Woody Allen."

Arabella unveiled the "pièce de résistance." No-one could resist *It's a Wonderful Life*. This was bound to make Mark question his choices, she thought as she loaded up the DVD player. She had carefully chosen the DVDs and all other activities on the basis that they involved and enhanced family time. Arabella also gathered the family gingerbread making set, the family monopoly game, and the family sized chocolate box. She was going to make this the best "family" Christmas, even if it killed her.

Arabella watched Mark out the corner of her eye as he focused on the movie. Out of nowhere, he started to sob, his breathing increasing rapidly. Oh my god, it was happening. He was having a heart attack! Arabella rushed to his side, hugged him and told him she loved him. He leant his head on her shoulder and muttered: "I'm sorry."

Arabella noticed he wasn't clutching his chest. Was he even dying? Of course not. It suddenly dawned on Arabella that her coward of a husband was having a panic attack. *Good*, she thought. Was this going to be how he responded every time he was reminded of their family? *About time you started regretting your bad decisions. An affair will have an effect on the body.*

She offered him water and stroked his brow. She hugged him

and led him upstairs so he could lie down.

"Lily, can you stay here whilst I look after Daddy please? He's not feeling well."

Arabella knew this was her moment. Her moment to remind her husband of what they had. She helped him onto the bed and lay down gently next to him, still murmuring words of encouragement. She started to lightly stroke his thigh and tummy, just like she had done in the past and lay her head on his chest. His heartbeat slowed down and he looked down at her as if he wanted to tell her something. He just lay there looking deep into her eyes but remained silent, not a word was spoken. It was as if the guilt was gnawing away his insides.

Mark closed his eyes deep in thought and Arabella knew she had him. She climbed on top of him, grinding up against him. They made love, eyes boring into each other. She told him she loved him, unable to ignore the flicker of sadness hidden beneath the smile he directed at her.

The other night was amazing.

Arabella tried to push Betty's words out of her mind. Mark still loved her! He just proved it and it was wonderful. Not exactly *Fifty Shades of Grey*, more ten shades of beige.

I miss you.

Again, Betty's words assaulted her.

We are soulmates.

Arabella, with a renewed energy, sat back on top of Mark, straddling him. Connecting, she leaned forward and reached underneath the side of the bed. Arabella pulled out a pickaxe, plunging it into Mark's chest and stabbing him again and again. Mark, completely taken by surprise, lay there motionless, not a sound emanating from his bloodied body. Arabella stood up with a satisfied expression, slowly wiping the blood from her hands and calmly placing the pickaxe back under the bed.

Okay, things got a little *Basic Instinct* there for a moment, but a girl can imagine, right?

Mark, relaxed and seemingly in the mood to talk, smiled up at her. Arabella changed tactics.

"How's work?" she asked him.

"It's fine." he answered.

"Did you have fun ice-skating the other day?"

Silence.

How would she know he went ice-skating if she hadn't read all his messages? Oh crap!

"The work outing you went on, like you do every Christmas. Was it fun?" *Please shut up Arabella, you're making it worse,* she told herself.

"Nope," Mark answered un-phased by her line of questioning.

Phew! That was close.

"You know how much I hate work outings."

Wow, an out and out lie! *Okay,* Arabella thought, *let's play a new game. 'How Many Lies Can He Tell This Christmas?'*

"You know we should try and get to the movies this Christmas, just you and me. *The Hunger Games* is supposed to be brilliant. Have you seen it?"

A very long pause...

"No."

Another lie!

"Oh good! Maybe we can see it when we get back."

She had seen the photo of the ticket stubs on his iPad. She never knew Mark could lie with such ease. She leant over and kissed him on the head.

"I'm so happy we're together for Christmas. I have a few special gifts for you."

Mark beamed. There it was. The old Mark. The old Mark that loved his crazy wife and who adored his family. She had succeeded in reminding him how important their family was.

Arabella: 2 Betty: 0

Arabella slipped downstairs. She knew Mark would be asleep in a matter of seconds. *Some things never change,* she thought.

Time for Phase Two.

Arabella flipped through the photos she had just taken of them all. A happy family home should be shared, shouldn't it? She uploaded the Christmas photos, turned the volume up on the festive music emanating from the radio and started to prepare Christmas lunch for the next day.

A few minutes later Mark stormed down stairs. "What do you think you're doing?"

Arabella stared at him in disbelief.

"What do you mean my darling?

"The pictures you put up on social media? I don't want people to see where we are or what we're doing!" he yelled.

Mark, catching his own words, lowered his voice.

"This is our private time and I don't want it shared with random strangers."

Arabella, repulsed by Mark's outburst, knew exactly what he meant. He didn't want Betty seeing happy family photos when he had told her about his failing marriage. He had obviously told Betty a bunch of lies and just wanted to cover his tracks. Well screw her and screw him! This was their marriage.

The vows were "I do." Not "I will, but only until I find someone else."

"Don't worry darling, I'll make sure there are no unflattering photos of you," Arabella said before running upstairs and sobbing into her pillow. She had never seen that side of Mark before. He looked terrified. Terrified that Betty would find out that he had lied and afraid Betty would see through his deception. She wondered if Betty's family had a hold over him that she didn't know about. Maybe Betty was pregnant and if he didn't agree to marry her after knocking her up, they threatened to "deal with him".

Arabella thought she had found a good man. A man she could trust implicitly. How would she ever explain all of this to Lily?

And if she couldn't trust men how on earth was she supposed to teach it to her daughter?

She had three days to make this marriage work, so refocusing her energy was an absolute priority. But first, she needed to know exactly what she was up against. Time for operation research. She sat with her phone on the toilet, knowing this was the safest place to look at google without being disturbed.

Arabella typed Betty Jones into the search bar... Her hands

shook. The anticipation of what she was about to uncover rattled her. She watched the circle of death go round and round and then stop. Twenty Betty Jones's? She retyped her name in again but added the names of Mark's friends. Bingo! She was getting good at this detective work, even if she had to say so herself.

No bloody way! An Absolution girl? Absolution was one of the 'It' magazines of London. Any girl gracing the pages of the magazine was single, sexy and wealthy. Or had a wealthy husband. She seemed to be the former. Yep, there she was in all her glory, with a group of friends that Arabella recognized. And she designed cards! Cards she decorated with vintage accessories she found on her travels. *How marvelous,* Arabella thought with disgust. She was a trust fund babe. No wonder Mark was all gaga eyed for this woman.

Betty was worry free and had no children. She could keep Mark in the lifestyle to which he longed to become accustomed. Was she even aware that her relationship with Mark was destroying their family? Or was Mark lying to her too? Arabella carefully considered how to proceed next.

She sent Alice the photo from the magazine.

"Thoughts....?"

"Still not as pretty as you," Alice replied immediately.

Arabella was far from convinced. This woman was living a carefree life, sleeping with her husband and had clearly no regard for the sanctity of marriage. Arabella's rising anger catapulted her to a place of no consequences.

She didn't just want her husband back, she wanted revenge.

Arabella didn't want to be this woman but the two of them had forced her into it. All she wanted was a simple, stress-free existence. In another life perhaps she and Betty could have been friends. It wasn't Betty's fault she had been misled by Mark. Mark couldn't have told her the whole story, surely? Another woman wouldn't knowingly do this to one of their own, would they?

Arabella thought about the pain she wanted to inflict on her treacherous husband. "Lily, Mummy's just going to have a quick bath, Ok? Then you must go to bed or Santa won't visit you?" she shouted out of the bathroom.

"Okay Mummy."

Lily was gloriously happy and innocently unaware of everything going on around her.

Arabella locked the door and ran the bath. She felt like a naughty schoolgirl, her tummy doing somersaults. She looked around the bathroom searching for a clue to aid in her revenge plan. Arabella's eyes locked onto something colorful.

Damn you to hell Mark!

She picked up Mark's toothbrush and twirled it in her hands, studying it closely. When did he find time to get an extra expensive electric toothbrush? He would whine continually about the unnecessary cost of this particular model but here he was in possession of one. Betty's influence no doubt, Arabella was sure of it. She fully submerged his toothbrush in the toilet bowl water before scraping it around the porcelain sides. "This is for cheating and this is for lying!" She dunked his toothbrush again and repeated the scraping in case she missed any grime the first time.

"And this is because you're a lying cheat!"

She heard Mark downstairs, probably on his phone. Lily used to always play on his mobile device but recently he changed his codes and told her it was solely to be used for work. He was quite adamant she couldn't touch it, which Lily couldn't understand. *Okay, just one more quick mix in the toilet bowl and then back on the side*, Arabella mused. *Third time lucky.*

As ridiculous as Arabella knew she was being, she couldn't help but feel slightly better. Having the knowledge that he would be cleaning his teeth with his new electric super deluxe expensive toothbrush later on tonight really delighted her. If Mark wasn't careful, she would do this every day of their holiday.

Arabella was emotionally mature enough to know her acting out was because she felt rejected and utterly let down. How could she compete with Miss Millionaire who never had to really work for a living?

We can work together and create a business, "cards and cafes".

Another message that punched her in her heart. They were supposed to be trying for a second baby this year. A thought that gnawed away at her insides.

Alice texted back, *I think you're so strong, keep on going, only three days to go. I'm here for you.*

God this was hard, but she had to keep on going.

Mark shouted from downstairs, "I know it's late but I want to go and check the slopes for tomorrow."

"We can't leave Lily," she shouted from the bathroom.

Arabella remembered the last time she was on the slopes. They had been on a skiing trip with all of Mark's friends and it had nearly ended in disaster. She had pretended she liked skiing and the cold, she would do anything to be with Mark. She had borrowed all the necessary skiing equipment from Mark's mum. Everyone had gone off without her as they were all avid skiers and Arabella had stayed back to take her first lesson. They all agreed to meet up for lunch later.

Arabella was exhausted from her first attempt at skiing and was looking forward to a rest and a steaming mug of hot chocolate. Mark popped up just before lunch and suggested they go off and explore. Arabella didn't want to sound wimpy or let him think she wasn't enjoying herself so she had half-heartedly agreed. They were utilizing the easy runs, Arabella just about coping, when they had found they had ventured off too far. Unfortunately, the only way down the mountain was on a red run, used by experienced skiers.

It was getting cold and dark and the slopes would be closing soon. Arabella looked down and almost fainted, tears welling up in her eyes. The slopes were getting icy as the temperature dropped and they were still far away from the resort. Arabella, convinced she was going to die and scared shitless, refused to move. Mark, terribly annoyed, had no choice but to go and find help. Arabella was so relieved as she heard the Skidoo. She had practically leapt onto the bike with the mountain guard as Mark skied down beside them.

Mark was tense and uncommunicative for the rest of the trip, and Arabella was sure she would never be invited on a ski holiday again.

Arabella hoped for better memories skiing this time, but it

already didn't appear that this was going to be the case. She saw Mark's wash bag lying on the side, his contact lenses in full view. She looked at herself in the mirror. She couldn't, could she?

Let's see how you cope without these little babies.

Now he would have to wear his glasses. He hated wearing those thick black rimmed glasses. He never felt quite as good looking wearing them. She smiled wickedly, grabbed all his lenses and tucked them away in the "cushion of doom."

A few moments later she heard Mark upstairs, getting ready. She felt a smug sense of satisfaction as she heard him brushing his teeth. He deserved it.

She walked back into the bathroom looking rather gorgeously festive, if she did say so herself. He tidied away his wash things and turned the bag upside down, looking for something.

"Do you know where my contacts are? I know I brought them."

"Nope, no idea I'm afraid."

"I can't find my bloody contacts," he moaned.

"Oh no! Lily sweetheart, bed time now. Come upstairs."

"Lily, have you seen my contacts?" Mark shouted urgently.

"No Daddy."

"You must have left them at home," Arabella said, hiding a smirk.

"I need them for tomorrow!" Mark replied, dejected.

Arabella felt sufficiently satisfied.

They put Lily to bed, smothering her with an abundance of kisses. The cabin was so perfectly located, they were two minutes from the slopes and the lifts. They could sit on their balcony and see the slopes and village.

The village was cute, unlike the Verbier types with big nightclubs and music blaring. It had a cozy family atmosphere, with a tall Christmas tree standing proudly in the centre of the village square. Arabella guessed there were probably about twenty cabins in the resort. Each cabin was lit with various coloured lights. It was like a mini Disneyland. It was peaceful. They sat on their balcony as the thick white snow fell. Arabella wore Lily's beanie as she hadn't dried her hair and didn't want to catch a cold.

They looked out over the dark slopes and Mark turned to Arabella and said, "Thank you for arranging this."

Arabella stopped herself from speaking. Her emotions were all over the place and she knew if she opened her mouth there was a strong possibility she would start wailing like a banshee. She put her arm gently around Mark and they stared up at the sky, enjoying the shimmering fresh snow falling around them.

"Come on, let's get you back inside. We don't want you catching a cold," Mark said lovingly.

As they walked back together Arabella felt like she was lost in the middle of a movie. Not an imagined movie but her movie, the movie of her life. Back inside, the fire roared whilst Mark made sure a guard was safely secure around it. Arabella prepared two cups of hot chocolate and as Mark sat down in the chair, she chatted about the Christmas day preparations.

They cuddled on the sofa like nothing had changed. They laid out Santa's treats for Lily, eating half the carrot and cookie. Arabella closed her eyes, making sure to capture the moment. It was perfect. This was a night she would never forget. Mark had actually not been on his phone for at least two hours. Arabella one; Betty nil.

TITANIC

Rose: "It's so unfair, Ruth."

Ruth: "Of course it's unfair. We are women, and our choices are never easy."

Arabella couldn't believe Christmas day had finally arrived and she was still in one piece emotionally. How had she managed not to implode over the last forty-eight hours, knowing what she did? It was like she was having an out of body experience and she had no control over her faculties.

If someone had told her last week she would be in this situation, she would have laughed out loud. Now she was expressing amusement but in a manic, psycho kind of way. They had gone to sleep the night before wrapped in each other's arms and had woken up with their bodies still enveloped.

They tiptoed downstairs to wait for a soon-to-be over excited Lily. Mark was wearing an incredibly un-fetching Superman onesie, at the request of Lily. Arabella had chosen her outfit carefully, making sure she looked like she hadn't really tried hard at all but totally had. She wanted an outfit from *The White Company* but her budget only afforded *Primark*.

Lily chose Santa outfits to wear later in the day. Lily was to be dressed as an elf, Mark Mr. Claus, and Arabella Mrs. Claus. Mark did not look his best at present. He looked uncomfortable dressed in his superman onesie. Arabella wickedly thought this would be the perfect time to take family photos. A great big boat load of them. She had already started her day by having a bit of fun disturbing Mark in the bathroom whilst he "showered."

She heard him on the phone whispering and when she fiddled with the door handle she noticed he had forgotten to lock the door. Taking full advantage of his faux pas, she bounded in without warning. Mark, taken by surprise, slipped and landed swiftly on his bottom, grabbing the shower curtain in the process. His phone, like a wet bar of soap, slid across the bathroom floor.

"What the…"

Arabella held back giggles.

"Just brushing my teeth, don't mind me."

Mark, naked and confused, reached for a towel, wrapping it around him. He reached for his phone as if it were a grenade about to explode.

That'll teach you, Arabella thought.

Arabella continued preparing the fire for Mark to light, adding to the quaint and cozy atmosphere. She heard Lily open her bedroom door and race downstairs. She was so excited, Arabella was sure she was frothing at the mouth.

"He came, he came!" Lily sputtered.

"Yes he did, my darling."

Mark, Arabella and Lily eyed each other, knowingly.

As soon as Lily had massacred her Santa presents, they made the usual family phone calls. Arabella had no desire to speak to Mark's parents or brothers as she had discovered in the messages that they had previously met Betty. Mark's dad had mentioned Mark's "special friend." And then to add insult to injury, Mark had replied to Betty that his father thought she was lovely. That hurt so bad. Arabella thought she may never recover from reading those words. Everything was one big lie! She wanted to scream from the rooftops that she knew about the affair, but she had to keep herself together for Lily's sake. After New Year she would tell Mark that she knew what he and Betty were doing. She couldn't wait! Arabella plastered a smile on her visage as they facetimed Mark's family.

Arabella loved Angela, her mother-in-law. She was sweet and kind and although not always available to help out, she understood the hardships of being a mom and how hard Arabella worked at making a home for Lily and Mark. Angela lived near London and they loved to visit whenever they could. The fire was always lit, cups of tea consistently available by the gallon and an abundance of chocolate digestives.

Friends had even remarked how similar Arabella looked to her mother in law, which was a great source of amusement to the rest of the family.

Lily, dressed in her elf costume, performed for them. Mark caught up in his daughter's pleasure, jumped around, acting silly. Arabella, lost in the moment and laughing uncontrollably, joined in, dancing. Arabella wondered if Betty would ever see this side of Mark, the real Mark, the Mark she fell in love with. The Mark who thoroughly enjoyed being with his family. It was a moment Arabella would treasure. She wanted to press pause on the remote control, so they could be stuck here, in this moment forever. They were happy, truly happy. It made Arabella wonder what stories Mark had told

Betty about their home life.

Arabella's stomach let out a loud gurgle. She realized she hadn't eaten a thing since she found out about Mark's affair. She knew subconsciously she was punishing herself.

"Breakfast is ready," Arabella called.

"Is it my favorite Mummy?" Lily beamed.

"Of course, my darling, our usual Christmas brunch."

Lily loved smoked salmon and scrambled eggs and it pleased Arabella to watch her daughter practically inhale an entire plate of it. Arabella pushed her food around with her fork, still unable to eat. She just couldn't. Her stomach was in knots. She felt waves of emotion threaten to engulf her and turned away every so often to stop herself from crying.

No, Betty. You will not ruin our family Christmas, especially if this is to be our last one. She had such mixed emotions. In one sense, she wanted this all to be over, but in another, she couldn't imagine it ending.

"You outdid yourself," Mark said, a grin on his face. He seemed genuinely happy. Arabella smiled weakly, hoping she wasn't imagining things again.

Arabella cleared away the empty plates and listened to Mark and Lily planning their ski route. She held onto the kitchen sink, looked up at her angels and prayed. Prayed that everything would be Okay. Prayed that this was all a nightmare she would wake up from very soon. She opened her eyes and saw Mark looking at her with an odd expression on his face. He came over, wrapped his arms around her and held her.

"Thank you for making Christmas so amazing. You really are wonderful."

She turned to him and without realizing it, the kitchen knife she was cleaning pushed deep into Mark's body. She stabbed him, repeatedly. She couldn't stop herself, she had had enough. She was at breaking point. Lily ran into the room screaming, "Mummy, Mummy, what's happening?"

Arabella stood, blood dripping from her knife and arm. She didn't mean to do it. What would she tell the police? She stared at Mark's lifeless body spread-eagled on the floor.

"I'm sorry officer, he ran into my knife. Ten times."

"Mummy! Mummy!" Lily called out, interrupting Arabella's day dream. "It's time to open the presents under the tree!"

Mark stood watching her. "You Okay? You look like you've seen a ghost?"

"All good, thanks."

Arabella busied herself with the dishes, trying to act like a normal human being.

Great! thought Arabella. She sat cross legged and passed the presents out. She smiled the most brilliant of all fake smiles ever, willing it to remain for this shit show.

And the Oscar goes to?

She stood to receive her award.

"I would like to thank my ex-husband. Without him, this would never have been possible. Without his lies and cheating, I would not have been able to so excellently portray a woman scorned."

"Thanks, Mummy!" Lily jumped into Arabella's arms hanging on for dear life. Arabella couldn't hold it in any longer. She burst into tears.

"Why are you crying, Mummy?" Lily said, concerned.

"I'm just so, so, so happy my darling," Arabella said, recovering.

C'mon Arabella, keep it together. She sat there silently seething as she watched her daughter open presents from her husband's mistress. An ache of tremendous proportions throbbed deep inside her.

Keep it together Arabella, she told herself. *Keep it together!*

As Lily continued unwrapping her presents, Arabella turned to her husband and said, "What a beautiful gift honey. Where did you get it from?" The messages from Betty flashed into her mind.

"I just picked them up the other day after work," he lied again.

You lying son of a...

Arabella had to stop herself from leaping onto his lap and strangling him.

"Lovely," Arabella contained herself.

"Now it's time for you and Daddy to exchange gifts, Arabella," Lily said.

Mark had wanted Arabella to paint him something special at her painting class. Arabella loved going to her class. It was a creative outlet and a safe space she desperately needed. Originally, she tried to paint specific things, overanalyzing her choices but then she let herself go and painted according to how she felt. It was liberating. They were pretty good if she had to say so herself. A gallery in

London had even enquired about them.

Mark looked at her as he opened her gift, thrilled by the painting Arabella had labored over.

"It's beautiful, thank you." He leaned over to kiss her. As he did, his phone vibrated.

It reminded her of the Jaws theme. The threat was imminent and there was nothing you could do to stop it.

Bugger you, Betty! You are welcome to him.

"Oh, it's just my brother," Mark lied again. "I'll call him in a bit."

This man's propensity for lying was about to send Arabella over the edge. God, how she wanted to chop off his deceitful tongue and flush it down the toilet.

Arabella stood to her feet, seemingly calm, and dusted herself down. She needed to do something before she started weeping again. She made her way upstairs to Mark's suitcase and carefully picked up each pair of pants he owned, gazing at them like they were her prized possessions. She grabbed a pair of scissors from her bag and made little holes in every one of them. She then took all his shirts and made holes under every arm. As she cut through his clothing, she found herself humming a song she had heard recently. It was from one of her favorite shows, *Nashville.*

"You've got the wrong song coming through your speakers, this one's about a liar and a cheater, didn't know what he had till it was gone."

As she went downstairs, she heard the front door slam.

"Where's Daddy?" she asked Lily.

"He's gone to call Uncle Tom," Lily replied.

Yeah, right! Arabella knew who he was really calling. He couldn't wait one more day to call her? It was Christmas for heaven's sake. Did this man really have no shame at all? Arabella checked herself. Enough was enough. She refused to continue like this. If he couldn't go through one day without calling her, especially Christmas day, she knew they didn't have a chance. It was over. Fighting to keep her family together had taken its toll on her. He obviously didn't care about the state of their marriage or about working it out for Lily's sake, so why should she?

She calmly made her way back upstairs to the bathroom, opened Mark's wash bag and removed his hair gel. She walked to the cushion of doom and deposited it there with the rest of his stuff. If he was going to be here then he could walk around with curly hair and wearing his glasses that he hated so much. Plenty more opportunities for flattering photos she could post on social media!

Arabella began preparing lunch and waited for Mark to return. She was used to standing by, wondering when he would be back from work, a night out, wherever. In fact, even the night she was in labour Mark couldn't understand that going with his mate for a beer might not be the best option.

She had started to feel strange that morning, with severe tummy pains. They continued throughout the day and when her neighbor popped over with some lunch, they took one look at her and made a face.

"You're in labour," she had laughed.

Arabella and Mark looked at each other, shocked. It was happening. It was finally happening.

The phone rang and Mark had asked his friend if he wanted to go out and get a beer.

"Are you serious, mate?" his friend replied.

"Why?" Mark answered, confused.

"Arabella's in labour."

It took a few sterner words from his friend before Mark relented.

There were countless nights when Mark had promised to come home at a certain time and kept Arabella waiting with a hot meal she'd lovingly prepared for her husband. He always had a milieu of excuses and soon Arabella accepted he would arrive at least two hours later than anticipated.

Today was about Lily, she reminded herself. Music was playing in the background, lunch smelled delicious and the house looked beautiful. Maybe not quite on par with Nigella's cooking but not bad. Not bad at all.

Mark pulled into the driveway. At least he was on time. One had to be grateful for small mercies, she thought. He bounded in, clearly ravenous. Lying constantly must certainly work up an appetite, Arabella mused. Mark needed to eat often or he got incredibly grouchy. Arabella wondered if is she should delay lunch just to annoy him, but Lily was starving so she got ready to serve. They sat down and Mark made a toast.

"Thank you, Mummy for a wonderful lunch and a wonderful few days."

"Yes, thank you, Mummy," said Lily smiling.

Arabella sat, dumbstruck. These weren't words from someone who didn't love their family. She was confused. She wasn't sure if she fully had a grasp on what was truly happening.

After a perfectly pleasant lunch pulling crackers and chatting to Lily about her presents and skiing in the afternoon, Mark told Arabella he would clear up. This was a ritual they tried to keep in place; whoever cooked was exempt from cleaning up after.

Arabella kissed Mark and went upstairs. She needed to know she wasn't going crazy. She remembered from one of Mark's messages that he may have shared his secret with a mutual friend. She emailed the woman in question:

Hi Sam, just wondered what Mark meant the other day when he said you were upset to hear his news? Has work been bad for him?

SEND.

Arabella sat and waited. Oh God, what if this caused a massive problem? She hadn't exactly thought this through. But desperate times called for desperate measures, she encouraged herself. It was pointless regretting it now, she couldn't dive into the web and pull the email back.

Suddenly her phone pinged. She looked at it, expecting it to be a reply from Sam. Instead it was a text from Mark saying, *"There's a problem at the office with Sam, I need to go out and call her."*

Oh crap. I've ruined it. Completely buggered it all up! Arabella hadn't wanted Mark to find out that she knew about the affair until after Christmas. Arabella panicked. She ran downstairs but it was too late. Mark had driven off before she could do anything.

If only she had kept her mouth shut.

Arabella tried her best to wait patiently but was not succeeding. What was she going to do?

"Mummy, can you come and play, please?" Lily asked as she spread her toys around.

Arabella couldn't concentrate. She kept pacing up and down the living room, stopping to look out of the window every so often.

"Not now my darling, Mummy doesn't feel very well."

Arabella found her phone and texted Alice. "*I've done something stupid.*"

Arabella waited for a response. Nothing.

She couldn't expect Alice to respond. It was Christmas day and it was unlikely anyone would be on their phones. Arabella's heart stopped as she heard Mark's car in the driveway. She took a deep breath and prepared herself for the fireworks.

As soon as Mark walked in, she confronted him, "Are you having an affair with Sam?"

Mark was so taken aback, he literally laughed out loud.

"Of course not."

"I'm so sorry darling. You spend so much time together, I don't know what came over me."

"It's ridiculous you thought we were having an affair! But I accept your apology."

Wow! So that's how you're going to play this. Arabella almost screamed. How dare he look at her like she was the lunatic for even considering he might be having an affair? That instant she decided she would never have him back, even if he begged her on his hands and knees. What man would let the women he was cheating on apologize for guessing the truth? This was too twisted and Mark was clearly no longer right in the head. For the first time, Arabella didn't see the man she loved for all those years. She looked him in the face, giving him an opportunity to own up to his mistakes, and he wimped out.

She was finally done.

Mark turned to Lily. "How about a bit more skiing before it gets too late?"

Lily was too busy playing with her new toys to get remotely enthusiastic. Arabella cajoled her along.

"Go on my darling, it will be fun."

"Will you come, Mummy?" Lily said.

"Of course." Arabella couldn't think of anything worse than trudging out into the snow, but since she knew it was probably the last time they would do anything as a family, she agreed.

They waited for Mark to get changed. He was worse than a woman and they had both joked about it for years. Unlike most women, it didn't take Arabella longer than two minutes to get ready. She didn't wear much makeup at all. Mark normally spent ages perfecting his hair and putting his contacts in. This time was quicker, he appeared, looking entirely unsexy with curly hair and black glasses.

Ah, the perfect Kodak moment, Arabella smirked again.

TEN THINGS I HATE ABOUT YOU

Bianca: "You don't buy black lingerie unless you want someone to see it."

Dressed in their ski outfits, they made their way up the slope, Lily already complaining about the cold. Arabella empathized with her daughter. It was bloody freezing! She found a spot to sit, with a clear view of them.

"I'll wait here my darling. Go on and have some fun with Daddy."

They both headed off, Lily dragging her heels behind her. Arabella began thinking about her life and all the decisions she'd made, leading her to this moment.

What if she hadn't married Mark? Or hadn't had Lily? Life without her wonderful daughter was incomprehensible to say the least, but Arabella couldn't help wondering how different her life could have been.

Lily pulled up next to her abruptly, snow flying everywhere. A somber look covered her face.

"Mummy, Daddy is looking at a photo on his phone of a lady. Who's the lady in the red dress?"

Oh crappity crap! Arabella wasn't prepared for this. Mark, you thoughtless prat. I mean, couldn't he be a little more careful?

"Mummy it wasn't you. And while we were up there, Daddy was on his phone all the time."

Arabella felt the heat rise up inside her like a simmering volcano. Deadly fumes were about to shoot out of her mouth, incinerating Mark if he showed up right now. How dare he do this to their daughter? Couldn't he just stay off the phone for one day? It was Christmas Day for goodness sake. She tried to remember her breathing technique from Lamaze class. In, out, in, out she breathed, slowly calming down.

"I don't know my darling." Arabella racked her brain for a suitable answer.

"Don't worry, it was probably just Aunty Rebecca."

Thank goodness Lily was always good at improvising.

Arabella, slightly pale, smiled weakly as Mark skied down beside them with a massive grin on his smug face.

As they returned to the cabin, Arabella quickly walked ahead, trying to figure out what to do next. Get him to confess once and for all, or keep this charade going? She needed to protect Lily. What was the best solution for their daughter?

As if in a trance, Arabella discussed with Mark their plans for the evening, the whole time looking at him as if he was the creature from the Babadook. As soon as she walked into the cabin, she reached for her notebook and started to write. All her emotions, her anger, her upset flowed out of her. She couldn't stop.

"Mummy I have another show for you," Lily interrupted.

"That's marvelous darling. How about we all get changed and then you can perform for us?" Arabella agreed, making a concerted effort not to show Lily how torn up she was about the Lady in the Red Dress.

Mark suddenly turned to Arabella. "I just remembered I said I would call my brother back in the UK."

Oh no, she thought. *You will not continue to make a mockery of me, of our daughter.*

"Why don't you just call him from here?" Arabella said, sweetly.

Mark, a little shocked, deftly recovered.

"Well I need to Facetime and we have no Wi-Fi."

He was right of course. Arabella was supposed to have fixed the Wi-Fi issue, but when Mark discovered Starbucks' Wi-Fi her plans had gone to pot.

"But it's too late now," Arabella countered.

Mark knew Arabella had a point and there was nothing he could do about it.

"Fine," he grunted. "I'll call in the morning."

For the next hour Mark sulked.

"How about you perform for us my darling?" Arabella hoped her daughter could at least turn his sour mood around. For Lily's sake that is. She herself was way beyond caring.

Lily sang for them again. She captured her heart so exquisitely, it was another moment Arabella would treasure for the rest of her life.

The days that followed Arabella found extremely difficult. Christmas was coming to an end and she was dreading it. She hadn't slept or eaten properly in days and she knew her angst was coming from somewhere much deeper. It felt like something inside was dying.

"I'm off for the Starbucks run," Mark said, again.

Arabella remained silent. She was too drained of energy to respond. However, she did muster up enough strength to hide his car keys. She may have given up on them ever being a family again but she was not going to make it easy for him to leave.

When she returned from the cushion of doom, she found Mark frantically searching for the car keys as if his life depended on it. It was a pathetic sight and reinforced Arabella's thoughts that this was most certainly not the man she married. He seemed weak and pathetically out of control somehow, under Betty's spell or thumb. Arabella couldn't quite decide.

Arabella imagined calling Betty.

"Hi Betty, it's Mark's wife, Arabella."

"Sorry who?" Betty replied.

"The woman whose husband you're having sex with."

"What? Oh, my goodness, I'm so sorry. I had no idea. I will end this immediately."

"That's perfectly Okay. I appreciate you doing that, thank you"

End scene.

But it would probably be more like:

"Hi, it's Arabella, Mark's wife."

"Oh hello," Betty replied snootily.

"You're sleeping with my husband. Is that all you have to say?"

"No. Hurry up and get divorced because I want to marry him and have his babies."

End scene.

Mark was still racing around like a mad man, hunting for the lost car keys.

"Arabella, Arabella?"

"What?" she almost yawned.

"Where are the car keys?"

In the cushion, with the charger, the contact lenses and the hair gel, you dumb Dodo.

"No idea, darling."

She spent the next twenty minutes half-heartedly attempting to help Mark find his keys. Strangely enough, to no avail. He was a mess.

It damn well served him right. All he had to do was be honest with her and they could move on.

"We have to find them eventually, otherwise we will be stuck here for days," he growled angrily.

Inwardly she laughed an evil Cruella De Vil laugh, but outwardly she couldn't help wincing in pain.

****

Arabella began focusing on their departure. She needed to get out of there. She had survived it all; the present opening, the texting, the sex and the lies, but now she needed this awful ordeal to end. She started to pack up the house, placing the presents and cards and decorations by the door.

Arabella nipped upstairs and grabbed everything from the cushion of doom and placed it in her case. She took out the keys and shouted downstairs.

"I've found them. They were up here all the time."

Arabella felt suspicious daggers flying from Mark, but she knew there was no way he could actually know. She acted as if it was all just a wonderful coincidence. "You can't have looked properly."

Arabella continued to pack whilst Mark began loading things in the car.

Her phone buzzed.

"How did it go?" It was Alice.

"I'm alive. More to the point Mark is still alive."

"See you when you get back?" Alice responded.

"Yes. Will call when settled." typed Arabella.

"Any plans for New Year?"

Arabella was so busy dealing with the nightmare that had become her life she had totally forgotten about New Year. *Time to put another plan in place*, she thought.

Arabella surveyed the precious holiday cabin and felt an immense sadness overtake her.

New Year was planned and arranged months ago, which was probably why it had completely slipped Arabella's mind. Originally, they were going to take the train from London and head to Disneyland Paris. But now she couldn't imagine spending the next five days with a man who literally made her skin crawl with his deceit and lies. How was she going to get out of this?

Then it hit her.

Chicken and rice…

A couple of years ago, Arabella had accidentally caused Mark to vomit. He was late for supper once again so she heated up leftovers from a couple of days earlier. Later that night, he ran to the bathroom and didn't leave for almost three days.

"Maybe it was something you ate at work? Lily ate the same as you."

But he knew she hadn't, which was when he guessed.

She apologized profusely and promised she would never do it again. Arabella felt terrible for days and really tried to make it up to Mark by cooking his favourite dishes. Well, she promised she would never make the same mistake again but she didn't promise she would never do it on purpose, right?

Her soon to be ex-husband might soon be her dead ex-husband. Oh dear Lord, what had Mark turned her into? She tried to laugh it off but she knew she was playing with fire. One wrong move and she could really make him very ill. She only wanted to incapacitate him then he would be unable to join her and Lily to see in the New Year. She felt somewhat justified because of everything he had put her through.

"I need to stop by a supermarket on our way home just to pick up a few basics," she said to Mark. "Why don't I drive us home as you drove us here, then you can sleep in the car?"

She knew if she drove, it meant that she was in control of the stops. She had no intention of taking a rest very often so he would not have time to phone Betty. She made sure Lily went to the bathroom before they left, but she knew Mark would need to stop at least an hour after they departed. He was like clockwork, needing to eat and using the facilities. After only twenty minutes Mark asked if they could take a break.

"Can we stop soon?" he asked.

"I'll pull over at the next petrol station."

It was so easy to get Mark flustered.

"We just passed another petrol station. Will you stop please?"

"Sorry, didn't see it," she said, sweetly.

The car needed petrol, so Arabella knew she had to pull in eventually but it gave her an odd satisfaction to play games with her cheating husband. It was a long journey to complete in one go but Arabella was determined to go for as long as she could and when she put her mind to something nothing would stand in her way.

Mark had a pained expression on his face. I mean really? Would Betty disintegrate if Mark didn't call her every few minutes?

"Here we go," smiled Arabella.

She pulled in to the upcoming petrol station, Mark seemingly about to burst.

"Go with Daddy Lily, just in case you need it."

Lily was half asleep but did as she was told and tried to chase after him. When they got back into the car, Arabella told Lily to stay with Mark whilst she ran into the twenty-four-hour supermarket to pick up a few necessities.

She bought the chicken and rice and packed the bombshell into the warm boot of the car. That should do the trick.

"OK, all ready?" Arabella got back in the car. Mark seemed to silently seethe for the rest of the trip, but she couldn't explain why. Arabella continued singing along to her Nashville sound track in her head and Lily slept.

By the time they got back home, it was late and Arabella put Lily straight to bed. Mark unpacked the car and again it seemed as if domestic bliss reigned once more.

"I'm going to just tidy up a bit down here."

Mark kissed the top of her head.

"Okay, night." He looked relieved.

Mark went up to bed and Arabella stayed downstairs to work her magic.

As Arabella prepared her husband's meal she hoped she and Lily would still be able to go and enjoy their day at Disneyland while Mark stayed at home feeling ill in bed. He deserved to feel ill after all she had been put through over the holiday. Her stomach had been in knots and now it was Mark's turn to feel some pain. She sliced the chicken and boiled the rice before going up to bed.

The next few days were filled with a weird normality as Arabella stood like a witch over her cauldron whilst Lily played with her toys. Arabella went to the doctor for a routine checkup and Mark continued pretending he was the dutiful husband, making Arabella's food preparations all the more satisfying. Was it going too far if she dropped the food on the floor? Or left it outside exposed to the elements overnight?

Perhaps.

It was like creating her own science experiment, Arabella thought. Cook, uncook, defrost, refrost, leave outside, and then place in the oven. She stuck it in the boiler, placed it in the freezer and then recooked it. Every night she hid it before Mark came back home. It still smelled like chicken so she knew she was safe. One night she had even placed it under his side of the bed. They had made love over a piece of chicken. When he went off to work in the morning, she removed it and began speaking to it, like it was a dead voodoo doll.

"Sorry you have to go through all of this. It'll be over soon, I promise."

BASIC INSTINCT

Nick: "Writing a book about it gives you an alibi for not killing."
Catherine: "Yes it does, doesn't it."

December 30th - The table was decorated and Arabella put on a special dress for the occasion. She chose a red dress that brought back particularly good memories. It was a dress Mark had bought her for an event which she wore when his company won an award. It was such a special night, she hoped he would remember the evening and his feelings for her. As Arabella fed Mark his dinner, she watched him savor every bite. It was like the last supper, only a hundred times better!

As he swallowed every mouthful, she said in her head, *That mouthful is for sending her flowers at Christmas, that mouthful is for buying the presents for your daughter with her, that mouthful is for calling her on Christmas day, that mouthful is for texting her on the slopes, that mouthful is for lying to your family, that mouthful is for sneaking off at work and having lunch with her.*

She counted down the list of awful things with every morsel he digested.

Mark turned to Arabella and smiled.

"It's delicious."

She hadn't planned for his next move. He turned to Lily.

"Lily, would you like some chicken?"

Fortunately, Lily was now a vegetarian. She looked at Mark as if to say, "Don't be stupid."

As Arabella turned to start the washing up, she heard over her shoulder Mark tell Lily he was going to give the leftovers to the neighboring cat. Like a slow-motion scene from *The Matrix*, she imagined pushing his hand away from feeding the cat and at the same time doing a double somersault. As the food fell to the floor she quickly jerked back to reality. Mark looked at her bewildered. Arabella, thinking on her feet said, "She's a vegetarian too!"

When Arabella went to bed that night she was plagued with mixed emotions. In one way, she was happy to have completed her mission. On the other hand, she was a little concerned that she may have killed him.

"That's five years for the chicken, five years for the rice and five years for preventing your husband from sleeping with another woman." The gavel hit the bench. "Take her down!"

Arabella loved courtroom dramas but this wasn't one she wanted to appear in. Now she panicked. Yikes! Bring on tomorrow.

New Year's Eve morning, the day of the Disney trip, Arabella woke to find Mark wasn't in bed.

"Mark, you there?" she shouted.

Maybe he had died and disappeared all in one go.

"He's on the toilet Mummy," came a shout from the hallway.

"Okay, my darling. Well, why don't you go and get yourself ready because our train's leaving soon."

Should she check on him? She couldn't really just leave him. He may have lost his liver and after all, she was responsible. After an hour had passed, she was just about to call emergency services when she realized Mark must be on his phone, as she could see he was "online." Had her plan worked? The uncertainty was killing her.

Her phone suddenly buzzed.

"*I feel awful.*"

She high fived the air "yes," and sent back a message saying, "O*h no, why?*"

She waited, hoping, praying. It buzzed again.

"*Because I'm making us late.*"

Arabella couldn't quite believe it. Nothing? Not even diarrhea? Bugger! Clearly her husband was made of sterner stuff. Her apparently well-laid plan failed miserably and she would have to continue playing happy families for the next few days. Urgh! She didn't know how much more of this she could take.

The train ride went by without a hitch. Arabella kept herself occupied by reading to Lily, and Mark did the usual tinkering with his phone. She managed to take a sneak peek over his shoulder when he wasn't looking and saw once again he was conversing with Betty. *Quelle bloody surprise,* she thought! He was either getting braver or more stupid, she couldn't work out which. *This trip is for Lily,* she kept telling herself. Encouraging herself was her only solace.

They pulled up to the park gates along with a million other people, it seemed. It was freezing and Arabella was pleased she had worn her massive winter coat and brought extra layers for Lily. Mark, however, stood there in what could only be described as clothing suitable for a summer's day at the beach.

"Why didn't you tell me it was going to be so cold?" he

snapped.

"Because I'm not your mother! Because you have a new woman in your life now and because I wanted you to suffer."

Instead she said, "I thought you knew.

Mark looked miserable.

"Here, borrow my scarf and hat," Arabella said, thinking Mark would say no. He surprised her by grabbing them and putting them on. *Oh well,* she thought. *More delightful photos for later.*

They spent all day cramming in as many rides as possible and finished their evening off with fireworks. It was well past Lily's bedtime by then.

"Let's go home. Lily is tired," Arabella pleaded.

Mark looked relieved at her suggestion. Sitting on the train on their return journey, Arabella thought about the letter she'd started writing at Christmas. The letter explaining how she knew about Betty. She would finish the letter that night. She planned on reading him the letter, laying out all his months of treachery before the New Year properly began. He wouldn't quite know what hit him!

It had flowed naturally from Arabella, summarizing what she had dealt with these last two weeks. As she sat on the train making its way across the English countryside with Lily fast asleep on her lap, she planned the day. She needed to make sure Lily wasn't around, perhaps Nicky would have her. She almost laughed out loud thinking of *Romeo and Juliet.* Instead of the parents reading the letter it was Arabella and she would make Mark take the poison and not her.

Yes, tomorrow was D- Day.

January 1st.

The phone rang early the next morning. No-one rings on January 1st so Arabella quickly answered it, worried a parent or family member might be in trouble.

Dr. Sung continued, "I'm afraid the cells have changed shape! Your check up from last week showed they have altered, Arabella. We need to get them removed now, let's make an appointment at the hospital for next week and get this sorted."

"Why is it suddenly so much worse?"

"Have you been under any undue stress recently? It can accelerate the cell growth."

Stress! Stress!

"Stress, well, it's Christmas, you know, family situation…difficulties." Arabella's high-pitched voice reached new levels. Every dog within twenty kilometres could hear her.

Arabella, numb, listened silently to the information. Mark had gone off to see "his brother." She was all alone. A preview of things to come, she wondered.

How was she going to afford this? The NHS would most likely help, but would they see her immediately? Mark was leaving her, he didn't care.

"Sorry how much?"

"£3,000," the doctor said.

Arabella must have misheard him. As always, she recovered nicely.

"Okay, thank you Dr. I'll see what I can do."

She texted Mark, *"I need to talk ASAP. Meet you at Shirley's."*

Shirley's was a little bistro in the village and she wanted to meet Mark on neutral ground. After the phone call with the doctor, she didn't want Mark in their home again. This was Arabella's day, this was the day to tell Mark she knew about Betty and what was going on. January 1st was the day to start afresh. The pretense of Christmas and New Year was now over and it was time for a dose of reality for Mark. She grabbed her bag, stuffed the letter inside and left on foot.

As she waited for Mark at *Shirley's*, she looked out of the restaurant window, feeling numb. She watched Mark walking toward the café, feeling an overwhelming feeling of animosity towards the man who had betrayed her.

Mark arrived, flustered. "Why on earth couldn't we meet at home?"

Arabella looked at him. His curling hair flopping over his eyes which betrayed the stress of living two lives.

"What was so important that you couldn't just call and tell me?" he continued.

Arabella wanted to tell Mark that she knew all about his relationship with Betty before she mentioned the hospital. Then he wouldn't feel obligated to do anything different or be part of her treatment if he didn't want to. Arabella wanted to release herself from the pain of dealing with Mark's lies to free herself to focus on her recovery. Now was the time to expose him for the person he had become, not the man she had married. Arabella took a deep breath. *You can do this.* She held herself steady. An eerie sense of peace came over. It was finally time.

"Where's Lily?" Mark snapped, irritated at Arabella's silence.

"She's with Nicki. Look, Mark, there is something I need to tell you."

Arabella took another deep breath.

You can do this.

A waiter appeared at the table. "Two glasses of wine please," Arabella ordered.

"I'm fine thanks," Mark replied.

"You'll need it, trust me," Arabella said.

Mark, now intrigued, urged her on. She pulled out the letter from her bag and began:

Dear Mark,

I have been writing this letter for the last few weeks. It may have seemed to you like we were having the best family Christmas but I have known something all along that has caused me huge upset. I knew your secret. Betty...

Arabella had summed up the courage and knew there would be no turning back. This was it. The final moment of their marriage. In a flash, something so precious was about to be destroyed. All the time together as a family was about to reach an abrupt and cruel ending. She then went on explaining in detail what she had endured over the last two weeks since she'd discovered the truth. It had nearly destroyed her.

Mark went pale, his face drained of blood. He looked down at the table. If only she could capture Mark's face at that moment. It was a sight for sore eyes! She would take a photo, keep it as a memento. Years later, whilst sitting with cousins and grandkids she would proudly turn the page and there would be Mark's face.

"And this was the day I told Mark I knew about his affair."

They would all laugh and comment on "the good old days."

"The doctor called today and told me I need to go in immediately to have pre-cancer cells removed."

The waiter arrived with their wine and placed it on the table.

"Thank you," Arabella said.

"Now will you be eating? Because I can run through the list of our specials…" the waiter continued.

"No, it's fine, thank you," Arabella said, silently pleading for her to leave.

"Are you sure, because they are really delicious."

"We are fine, thank you!" Mark shouted at her, shocked by his own outburst. The waiter scurried off.

Mark and Arabella continued in silence.

"How do you know?" was all he could muster.

He looked scared and somewhat bereft. Arabella looked at his now small frame and wondered if all the lies had taken a toll on him. Perhaps he really was sorry for what had happened. She felt slightly comforted by the notion, suddenly in control for the first time in two weeks.

Mark looked her dead in the eye and said, "I want a divorce."

This was it? Her marriage was finally over? No tears? No lengthy apologies? It had been that easy for him?

Even knowing their marriage would end today, she hadn't expected to feel so utterly shaken. Arabella needed to leave before she crumbled into a big heap on the bistro floor, humiliating herself in the process.

She knocked back the glass of wine and said calmly.

"Please don't come back to the house tonight."

She stood up and walked out.

DIRTY DANCING

Johnny: "Nobody puts baby in the corner."

Johnny: "I'll never be sorry."
Baby: "Neither will I."

The next day Lily was told Daddy had to go away on business, so she kissed him goodbye and ran up to her room to play. Arabella helped him pack, he surprisingly didn't have much stuff. As he stood on the porch facing her, he seemed torn whether to kiss her or make contact of any kind. He leaned forward and as he did, Arabella turned and closed the door behind her. And then he was gone... ten years together, eight years of marriage and now she was on her own, left to pick up the pieces of her failed marriage.

As if Alice instinctively knew how much Arabella needed comfort, the phone rang.

"I'm coming over! Don't do anything till I get there." Alice said.

Arabella sat waiting in her home that now felt strangely unfamiliar. Everything was tidy, Mark's things no longer lying absentmindedly everywhere. All his things would never be left on the side again. She would never again complain to him about his mess. Sadness engulfed her like a heavy veil, the thing she feared finally a reality. It dawned on her that no one knew what was happening. She hadn't even spoken to her in-laws. She grabbed her laptop, wrote an email and before she knew it, sent it to everyone, including Betty.

"So, Christmas wasn't as much fun as we thought it would be. I know you are all aware Mark has a new girlfriend, which of course was news to me, his wife of eight years. After finding out about the affair, I have asked him to move out today, which he has done. Lily is unaware of the situation and Mark has asked me not to tell her until he sees fit. Please do not discuss this with her until we deem an appropriate time.

Signed,

Arabella.

Oh and Betty,

I hope you will be very happy with my husband.

Arabella.

SEND.

Arabella realized that sending an email when she was feeling so completely desolate and abandoned probably was not the best idea, but she was so angry. No explanations, no discussions, no nothing. How was she going to go into hospital and take care of Lily at the same time? Of course, her friends would help, but it wasn't a question that even crossed Mark's mind.

The front door opened and Arabella couldn't contain herself any longer. She burst into tears, weeping uncontrollably. Alice wrapped her arms around her and just held her. Arabella had kept her emotions in check for so long, it was time to let it all out. She sat there crying, all the pent-up pain pouring out. Alice went upstairs to check on Lily. She put on a DVD for her and told her Aunty Alice was downstairs if she needed anything.

Alice made Arabella a cup of tea and sat and listened whilst Arabella told her what had happened with Mark up until now.

"You know us girls are here for you, right?"

This had made her cry even more.

Next week came altogether too quickly. Mark insisted he was going to tell Lily and wanted to set up a time at the house to do so. He didn't offer to take Lily for the day which was typical of him, she thought.

Minimum input: maximum output. That was Mark.

Arabella went in to hospital the next day and came back to bouquets of flowers. The following day Arabella waited for Mark to turn up for his appointment with Lily and as usual, he was running late. She thought she would pass the time by checking her emails and when she did, she noticed one from Lily's godmother. This was the first of their friends to acknowledge their break up, and it was a hard pill to swallow. No denying it anymore, this was real and there was no going back now. If Lucinda knew, then everyone would know.

And soon.

Arabella took a deep breath. The room began spinning and she tried to steady herself, reciting the mantra from one of her books. "Breathe and see, breathe and see, breathe and see."

She looked in her diary and realized it was only two days until Mark's birthday. What did one do in this situation? Was she still meant to send him a card? Lily loved making cards and would shower Arabella with them throughout the year. Just because she and Mark were no longer together didn't mean she had to be impolite. She would still send him something, via Lily perhaps.

His car pulled up outside. He rang the doorbell and Arabella answered it. It felt particularly weird letting Mark into his own home. The home he lived in with them as a family only a few days ago. Awkward greetings were exchanged followed by Mark predictably asking Arabella what she thought was best. Couldn't Mark work this out for himself? Arabella was still in shock and finding it difficult to think. She'd just come out of hospital for goodness sake.

"Probably not having the affair in the first place," she said coolly.

"Arabella, that's not helpful," he snapped.

She knew he had a point, but she was still angry.

"Well, what do you want me to say?" she continued.

"I'm trying to do what's best for our daughter," he added.

"Oh and I'm not?" her voice rose to a shrill.

This wasn't going anywhere. She was letting him get to her. *Be the bigger person, Arabella. You can do it.* Arabella thought it best if they went for a walk to explain to Lily that Daddy didn't love Mummy anymore and was in love with someone else. She didn't think Lily needed all the details but Mark wanted to be honest.

Really? Now you want to be honest?

Lily bounded down the stairs.

"Lily, daddy's here. Come, boots on please."

She hugged her father. "Hi Daddy."

"There's my munchkin," Mark affectionately said.

"How's work Daddy?"

Arabella and Mark, uncomfortable with this line of questioning, shuffled around in silence.

"Family hug?" Lily said expectantly.

Arabella was in no mood for a "family hug."

"Of course, munchkin," Mark agreed.

Mark thrust himself at Arabella giving her no choice but to hug him. He smelt different. He was wearing new clothes, and she noticed his new hairstyle. Hold on, that was a new watch. Where was the watch she had given him from their wedding? Mark caught Arabella's gaze as she stared at the watch. Lily examined it too.

"It's all sparkly, Daddy!"

"Yes, it's from a friend. A birthday gift."

He'd replaced his old watch with a newer model just like he had done with Arabella. Another item tossed aside and swapped so easily for him.

They slowly walked outside to the brook that ran across the bottom of their lane. Lily jumped in and out of puddles, having a ball. She looked so happy. Arabella was terrified at how she might respond to Mark's confession.

"Come and sit down next to Mummy and Daddy, munchkin," Mark asked lovingly.

Lily, excited about the prospect of big news, raced into her Daddy's arms.

"Mummy and Daddy are going to live in different houses for the moment," Mark said softly.

Lily eyed them both, a little perplexed.

"But Mummy, what about when I want to see Daddy?"

"Daddy is going to have a new house now."

"But he has a house already."

"Daddy needs to stay in his new house for a little while."

Arabella looked to Mark for support, a reassuring word, something, but he remained tight lipped. Arabella continued to explain that Daddy was moving out and that things were going to be different from now on. Lily, still trying to make sense of it all, lowered her head, crushed. Arabella held her as she cried.

They walked back to the house, Lily clasping tightly on to Arabella's hand. Mark offered her his other hand but Lily refused to take it.

"I should probably go then," Mark muttered, feeling uncomfortable.

Arabella couldn't wait for him to leave.

"Yes, that's probably best. I'll call if anything happens."

"Lily, can Daddy have a hug?" Mark urged Lily to embrace him.

Lily didn't move. She looked at Arabella for permission, breaking Arabella's heart in two.

"Best you go, Mark," Arabella said.

She felt sad for Mark as this wasn't the reaction he obviously expected but he had no choice but to accept it.

"I'm sure she'll feel different in the morning."

Mark left Lily and Arabella bent down and hugged her daughter tightly.

Arabella attempted to go through Lily's usual routine before bed, but she was looking up at Arabella with an odd expression on her face.

"Mummy, some of my friends' parents don't live together and they got a, a...d..."

Arabella knew she wanted to say divorce but couldn't, so Arabella shouted.

"Wonderful idea! Yes, let's get a dog!"

Lily beamed.

Arabella lay in bed later, flabbergasted at her reaction. A dog? What a stupid idea. They couldn't take care of an animal. Certainly not now! She would have to distract Lily and hope she moved onto something else quickly.

The next morning Lily ran into Arabella's bedroom and jumped on top of her. She seemed oblivious to Mark and the devastating news from yesterday, only remembering Arabella's idiotic suggestion.

"Can we have a white one please?" she said almost hyperventilating.

"Huh?" Arabella, barely awake, rubbed her eyes.

"A white dog. Can we have a white dog mummy, please?"

Arabella looked up at the ceiling, hoping God might give her a way out of this. She looked at her daughter bursting at the seams with joy and excitement, and she had no energy to refuse or object.

"Of course my darling."

What was Mark going to say when he found out? Hold on, it didn't matter, did it? He no longer had anything to do with her daily decisions, right?

"OK we'll look into the dog situation later but for now I need you to do something for daddy. It's his birthday so you need to make him a card like you always do."

Lily looked at Arabella. "No, I'm not speaking to him," she said, turning around and marching back into her room.

Great, Arabella thought, *I'm sure I will get blamed for that.*

"Lily please!" Arabella jumped out of bed, running after her daughter.

"No, he doesn't deserve a card or a present," Lily said adamantly.

Lily could be determined at the best of times. *I wonder where she gets that trait,* Arabella thought. But she knew there was no point arguing with her when she was like this. She walked down the hallway to make a cup of tea and carefully considered her options. Arabella wanted things to continue as normal as possible for Lily. She decided she would make the card for Mark herself. She took out the card and pens and tried her utmost to recreate something Lily would think of. Arabella soon discovered making a card that looks like it's been put together by a nine-year-old was exceptionally difficult but very therapeutic.

She placed it in an envelope then realized she didn't know Mark's new address. It was still a mystery to her. She stood up and WOAH... Arabella sat back down again, feeling woozy and off centre.

"Oh my goodness." She tried to regain her balance but before she knew what was happening, she threw up, everywhere.

"Mummy!" Lily screamed as she came into the kitchen.

"It's okay my darling, mummy's not feeling very..." Before she could finish her sentence, she threw up again. She attempted to lift her head but failed miserably. Arabella needed help, but who could she call?

"Lily go and bring Mummy the phone."

"Mum," Arabella cried down the phone.

"My darling I'm on my way," Sarah replied.

Her mother knew Arabella well enough to know that her daughter was in dire straits. Sarah adored Lily and loved having her stay over.

"Can you go and pack a few things please to take to Sou Sou's," Arabella croaked.

Arabella's mother didn't want to be called Granny or Grandma as it had made her sound so ancient! They all agreed on Sou Sou. Arabella sat in bed watching helplessly as Lily packed her things.

"Teddies, books, toys, DVDs," Lily ran through her belongings.

"How about some clothes?" Arabella whispered.

"Nope. Sou Sou will buy me some clothes," Lily insisted.

Arabella was far too weak to argue.

Sarah deposited Lily in the car and left a week's supply of chicken broth in the fridge for Arabella. The house was eerily quiet and she wondered if she had made the right choice. She wasn't altogether sure she would survive the next week, let alone the next year. Lily wouldn't talk to Mark and Arabella didn't want to talk to Mark. How on earth had her precious little family come to this? She lay on her bed sobbing as her phone rang and text messages and emails flooded through. She vaguely remembered hitting the green button on her phone by mistake, possibly accepting a phone call. She heard a voice from someone who sounded something like her lying, cheating husband.

"Where's Lily? I want to talk to her."

Arabella, unable to lift her head from the bed to explain anything, closed her eyes and disappeared into the warm, safe vortex of sleep. Her dreams began…

She was lying in a hospital bed, like in the movie *City of Angels.* She looked surprisingly well for a person on her death bed, she thought. Well, apart from the number of tubes coming out of her mouth. She heard the nurse talking to Mark.

"I am so sorry sir. We did everything in our power, the prognosis does not look good."

Mark responded, "If I had known leaving her for Betty, that stupid, fat, old girl (it was Arabella's dream, okay?) would have amounted to this, then I would never have left this beautiful, intelligent and incredibly young-looking woman, the mother of my child."

Mark bowed his head in sorrow, tears streaming down his now crater face. As per usual, it wasn't just Arabella's family in the room, devastated to see her in such a state, but Gerard Butler, Brad Pitt and Bradley Cooper were also gazing at her lovingly. Bradley took Arabella's hand in his when suddenly a loud long beep came out of nowhere. *Oh God, I'm dying,* Arabella thought. The noise got louder and louder, until…

Oh crap! It's the doorbell. Arabella almost wept again, knowing she was not still locked away safely in her dream. She dragged herself to the door and opened it. Alice greeted her with DVDs and chocolate.

"Danks." Arabella muttered.

"That's okay, I thought you might need some TLC," Alice replied.

"I'm dokay," Arabella forced out through her congested nose. Her one saving grace was Bradley Cooper couldn't see her looking like this.

"You OK? We've all been trying to contact you," Alice said, concerned.

"I've not been looking at my phone. I wanted to keep off it."

"Anything you need, we are all on call. We have taken shifts." Alice smiled.

Arabella knew she wasn't joking. This was what the girls did, they rallied around to support each other.

"What are you doing?"

"Just lying in bed feeling so ill. You want to come in?"

"No, I best not. Don't want to catch what you've got," Alice said.

"A broken heart?"

Alice looked at Arabella. "It gets better, promise."

Alice blew Arabella a kiss. She closed the front door and Arabella sank to the ground. Alone. Crying into her lap.

SHAWSHANK REDEMPTION

ANDY: "Get busy living, or get busy dying."

It had been ten months since the great discovery of Mark's indiscretion. Arabella managed to struggle her way through every emotion possible, from uncontrollable sorrow to blinding anger. She still had a long way to go but at least she was heading in the right direction. She turned to the record player and thumbed through her choice of vinyl. She pulled out Dolly Parton. This always helped to lift her spirits. Each day Arabella wondered what the soundtrack to her life would be. Arabella let herself go, getting lost in the rhythm. It only seemed like yesterday that she heard the words, "I want a divorce."

She remembered some of the darker moments, like the night after she confronted Mark when she had sat and cried for what seemed like days. She had recorded a message for Mark on her iPad and sent it to him. She hadn't remembered she'd done it until the next morning. Her deep regret and abject humiliation were accompanied by a blistering alcohol-fueled headache. But apparently the Lord was watching over her because when Arabella clicked on the YouTube link to face her drunken self, it hadn't seemed to have uploaded. Thank goodness.

It might have been a cathartic experience if she could actually remember it, but at least it wasn't there to prove she was having some sort of mental breakdown. Apart from the occasional freak outs, she found ways to cope. She wasn't entirely sure how they would sort out their finances or how the future would pan out, but it was becoming easier with the consistent support from her friends. She was looking forward to a complete and utter sort-out of all their belongings tonight. Lily was staying at Sou Sous. Alice and the girls would be arriving soon.

The doorbell rang as she considered what snacks she could provide for her confidantes but as she opened the door and they all piled in with bottles of wine, chocolate, food and lots of empty bags she knew she had nothing to worry about. Alice had more bags than all the women put together. They all glanced at her suspiciously.

"What? I love Arabella's things and they'll be useful for my costumes!" Alice smirked.

"You're a piranha. You know that, right?" Nicki joked.

The girls laughed. They knew how passionate Alice was about her craft – costumes, costumes, costumes!

They sat and drank half the wine before even considering making their way upstairs. Jen turned to Arabella and said three words she hated hearing.

"Time will heal, Bella. You've made a great deal of progress already."

If she heard that sentence one more time, she would bloody well kick time right up the backside! The mending process was going a lot slower than she had hoped and Arabella's heart felt far from healed. Would the scars always remain, she wondered? The worst part was knowing Mark's heart seemed to be as good as new. Inevitably he had Betty to kiss it all better. *NO, must not be cruel! I must be kind.* Although she was getting better at it, she was still a work in progress.

The barrage of emails she received from Mark when he was bored or Betty was away didn't help matters.

"I know it takes time but I'm fed up! I despise the looks of pity I still get when I'm walking around the village. I wish I could start a new life." Arabella said to her friends.

They all nodded sympathetically.

"If I'm bored hearing about my own divorce, how must everyone else feel? They must be sick of me. I'm sick of me!"

They smiled, knowing that she was gaining more strength as the weeks passed by.

"Well let's start sorting then," Jen chimed.

The girls all looked at each other as if they were harboring a huge secret.

"Go on," Jen nudged Nicki.

"What's going on guys?" Arabella asked, confused.

"Well, we were all thinking that perhaps your house isn't the only thing that needs sorting. It's time to address your Facebook account.

Arabella looked horrified.

"What do you mean?" Arabella was not prepared for this.

"Well, you're still friends with Mark and you really shouldn't be," Alice continued.

"We want to help you terminate your friendship now," Jen said.

Arabella knew they had a point. She just wasn't sure if she was ready. Ever since she saw a photo of Mark and Betty out at a party on Facebook she knew it was time. She just didn't have the courage to pull the plug.

"Can we have one more look before we cancel it?" Alice begged.

They grabbed their wines and made their way up to the office. Arabella chuckled. *This might actually be harder than the divorce itself,* she thought.

"But what if I don't know who Lily is getting involved with?" she wailed, hoping her friends might change their minds.

"If it's important, I don't think you'll get it off Facebook honey." Alice set the record straight. "And besides, it doesn't make you feel any better knowing what the two of them are up to on a day-to-day basis."

Again, Arabella knew they were right. Only the other day she had seen a photo of them skiing, followed by a photo of them at someone's wedding, followed by a photo of them holding balloons with their initials. Some sort of birthday celebration. It was too painful to keep looking.

The girls huddled around Arabella, holding hands in solidarity to help her to sever the toxic connection.

"Oh God, this is harder than I thought," Arabella bellowed.

Mark.

UNFOLLOWED.

One down, only a few more to go. Arabella's courage grew by the minute.

"What about all the two- faced friends? Do you really need them in your life?" Alice said.

Sadly, it turned out, many of their mutual friends knew what Mark was up to before Arabella had known. Nope, they had to go too!

As she hit UNFOLLOW, one after another their information disappeared. Stories, photos, lives of so-called friends disappeared into the internet ether. A huge weight lifted off her shoulders.

"I had a friend whose son became friends with the ex and his family on Facebook so she could always spy on him," Jen said.

Arabella was shocked. Okay, not shocked per se. She actually thought it was really smart. However her days as a professional sleuth were over and anyway, Lily was too young to have a Facebook account, so that would never work.

She knew Mark didn't care whether they were friends on Facebook or not. In fact, he told her in no uncertain terms he would prefer it if they weren't connected. *Your wish is granted, your royal twit!* Arabella giggled at the absurdity of it all.

The girls, now raucous, tried on all of Arabella's clothes, parading themselves up and down the stairs. Arabella had lost nearly two stone in weight since the "Divorce Diet". The inability to eat and sleep for hours on end probably didn't help matters.

"So, are you going on one of those single mummies dating sites?"

The girls all gaped at Jen's outburst. Did she not have an off switch?

"No, why would I be on one of those?" Arabella replied.

Then it hit her.

She was a single Mum.

Oh dear God! It sounded awful. Like a has-been. A bizarre, extinct creature that would never have sex again. Single dads, on the other hand, didn't sound so bad at all. Women, in general, loved single dads. Single Mums, not so much. Might as well hide in her closet now and stay in there for eternity.

"I'm not sure it's my thing, to be honest," Arabella replied.

"Come on Bella! It'll be fun. You don't want those pipes of yours getting rusty, huh?" Jen added.

They all laughed in unison.

"Okay enough, enough, I get it! You want me to move on. I'm there already, Okay?" It seemed like the perfect moment to tell them. Arabella braced herself. She looked calm as a quiet hush descended on the group of friends. "Ladies, I've decided to go away."

"What, where?" Jen shouted in excitement.

"To LA. I need a change and it's almost Christmas, which is obviously a difficult time for me. I think it'll be good to take Lily away. I know it seems far, but I need to go as far away as possible. Something that we've never experienced as a family."

The girls hugged her, tears flowing. Arabella was touched. She hadn't expected them to be so supportive.

"I'll be back though, I promise."

The doorbell ringing unexpectedly cut them off mid hugs. It was so late. Who on earth could it be? Arabella ran down the stairs and looked out the door. Oh my god it was Colin, Mark's very good-looking cousin. What on earth did he want?

"What should I do?" she asked the girls.

"Answer it," they all giggled.

Arabella pulled the door open, taking Colin by surprise.

"I'm sorry I didn't know you had company, I'll come back another time." He turned to run.

"No, it's all good Colin! We were just going weren't we girls?" Alice nudged them all.

"Were we?" Jen replied, oblivious.

The girls fell out of the house sniggering like a bunch of hyenas. Arabella turned around just in time to notice the state of her house.

"I'm so sorry the place looks awful, I was having a clear out."

"I can see," Colin answered softly. "I can help."

"No, it's fine, honestly. I can finish in the morning."

Arabella caught a glimpse of her disheveled appearance as she walked past the mirror into the sitting room. She was horrified! Her hair looked like it hadn't been brushed for days, her top was covered in red wine and she had masses of chocolate stuck in her teeth.

"I'd like to help, I'd like to, really," he added.

Arabella smiled with her mouth shut. "I am just going to nip to the toilet, I won't be long. Please sit down."

Colin sat as Arabella quickly ran upstairs to try and repair the mess.

When she returned Colin had already started to carve out some floor space amongst the piles of clothes strewn everywhere. Arabella was secretly thrilled. She forgot how nice it was to have male company in the house. He helped her with the washing up, not saying much. It felt relaxed and comfortable.

"I'm sorry I haven't been over to see you before now," Colin said.

"I understand. You're Mark's cousin. It's a difficult situation for us all."

"Yeah, well, I wanted to tell you I think it's terrible what Mark did and I'm here if you need anything."

Colin leant over and kissed her. Not an 'I'm Mark's cousin' kiss but a full-on kiss. Arabella didn't pull away.

She couldn't believe it. Mark's cousin? There was no reason for her to feel guilty. Arabella needed this. One night to just be a woman. Not an ex-wife or a mother, but a woman. It was spontaneous, in the moment and caught Arabella completely off guard. This would be her first sexual experience since Mark, and boy she was ready. They made love in the sitting room, on the stairs and then finally in her bed. They lay in each other's arms, entwined for hours, touching, exploring. Arabella fell into a deep slumber, gloriously satiated. This was their little secret and no one would ever find out.

The next morning Arabella had woken to a note from Colin on her bedside table. It read:

"I know things are complicated for you but I loved last night and I'll always be here for you. Yours, Colin."

Arabella, high as a kite from all the endorphins, felt rejuvenated from being with Colin. She floated out to the mail box to collect the post. *Knight and Law.* Oh God, the lawyers! She had accepted the divorce would eventually go through, but perhaps she unconsciously still held onto a small glimmer of hope Mark wouldn't go through with it.

She slowly opened the envelope and yep, there it was. The decree nisi. God, she really couldn't deal with this now. She refused to ruin the memories of her wonderful evening last night with a legal nightmare so she stuffed the letter in the top drawer alongside everything else. She didn't want that post to ruin her memories of last night.

Sipping her cup of tea, her phone buzzed.

"So how was last night?" Alice asked.

She knew the others would be just as curious. *"Tell you later."*

She looked out of her window and visualised herself in LA. She imagined looking across the calm, cool water, past the palm trees and through the marina in the harbor.

That is where I'm supposed to be, she thought. *The next chapter in my life.*

Her night with Colin had marked another tie severed from Mark. She felt equipped with a new-found determination. Arabella, more courageous than she'd ever been, knew she could do anything she wanted. She would no longer allow anyone to hold her or Lily back from their best life. They had a dazzling future to procure. Arabella, who was aware more than ever, recognized that happiness was not being turned on by the men in your life, but it was being turned on by yourself. Adrenalin pulsated through every inch of her.

Los Angeles, we're coming to get you!

What did she have to lose?

AMERICAN PIE

Jim: "She's gone, oh my god, she used me, I was used. I was used, cool."

It was a week before Christmas and their flights to LA were nearly upon them. As Arabella packed up the house, a mixture of emotions washed over her. She looked around at the boxes filled with their effects.

She still couldn't believe they were going on a three-month trip to LA. She had no idea what they were going to do exactly when they got there but she wanted this Christmas to be special for Lily, as it was the first one without her father. Mark had chosen to spend Christmas with Betty and her family.

It was important to Arabella that her daughter had wonderful memories to look back on. Memories that could hopefully eclipse the brutality of divorce. She never wanted Lily to ever feel responsible for her parents ending their marriage and Arabella would spend the rest of her life making sure of that.

Arabella's lawyer told her she could either stay in the house and take on the mortgage, or they could sell it. She didn't want the hassle of paying for a mortgage and wanted a new home for her and Lily anyway. The "for sale" sign had been up for almost a week and there was already a great deal of interest in the property.

The phone rang.

"Hi darling, it's your mother."

"Hi mum."

"How's it going?" she asked.

"I should be done by end of tonight I think," Arabella replied.

"Great! I'll be down this weekend to pick up the last of your belongings. I've made extra room in the garage for storage."

"Thanks, mum," Arabella replied.

"Well, I'll let you get back to packing. I'm so proud of you, honey."

Arabella felt proud of herself too. Mark hadn't seen Lily in almost six months now. He made a few half-hearted attempts in the beginning but after Lily refused to see him, he stopped trying. Now communication between Mark and Lily was almost non-existent. A fact she knew was upsetting Lily, even if she pretended otherwise.

Arabella recognized she would have to tell Mark about their trip being slightly longer than originally planned, though she was not looking forward to the prospect of telling him. Although Mark had plans with Betty for Christmas, it was just like him to create an issue where there wasn't one.

She messaged him:

As you know we are going away for Christmas and it might possibly be for a bit longer. She had discussed her plans with her lawyer and as Lily was always with Arabella, she had been told there would be no problems legally. Of course, Mark would have an opinion as he had an opinion on everything.

His current bone to pick with Arabella was the fact that he was desperate for Betty and Lily to meet. Arabella had to constantly explain Lily didn't want to, but he continually fought against her.

This was not out of spite, as Mark would so love to believe. It was purely out of the desire to protect her daughter. Until Mark and Lily's relationship was back on track and Arabella believed Lily felt safe and secure, she knew Lily did not want to see Mark or Betty at this time. It was in Mark's power to change his relationship with Lily, but he needed to start putting in the effort.

She was still wrangling with Mark about finances but when the courts resolved it, she and Lily were free to be exactly who they wanted to be.

A couple of nights before they were due to leave for LA Mark was expected to come over to say goodbye to Lily. Arabella was still pottering upstairs.

"Okay my darling, can you just get yourself ready for bed? Daddy will be over in an hour."

"Arabella, I don't want to see him."

"I know my darling but we are going away for a few weeks so we must say goodbye to him, okay?" Arabella insisted.

Lily skulked off to the bathroom to brush her teeth, leaving Arabella to wonder if she was making the right decision to go away. What if the person who bought her house was really Jude Law from *The Holiday* and she was missing out on meeting Mr. Right? Her cottage always reminded her of the cottage in the film and well, who didn't want to be Kate Winslet? After all, she too was risking everything and heading out to LA.

Arabella's phone buzzed. A message from Mark to say he was here. Arabella's stomach involuntarily lurched. How could her body still be reacting to this man? She was over him, right? It had been months since she'd laid eyes on him, this could not be happening. Not now. She made her way to the front door, but she couldn't open it. She was frozen, almost paralyzed. Arabella could feel her eyes well up with tears. *Oh no you don't! You will not blubber over this bastard.* And then the unthinkable happened, she cried. She cried because she knew she had to see him. And when she laid eyes on him all she could see was Betty. *Arabella, you are a strong woman,* she thought. *You will not let this man derail you. Not when your new life is just around the corner waiting for you.* Arabella wiped her tears, propped herself up and opened the door. Mark, in a cashmere jumper and penny loafers, stood alongside a Mercedes soft-top sports car. He looked different. Betty had done a complete overhaul on him and she wasn't exactly sure it was for the better. *Must not be a bitch,* Arabella chanted in her head. *Must not be a bitch.* His appearance was no longer her concern.

As they embraced awkwardly, Mark's familiar scent lingered and they held onto each other for a tad longer than soon to be divorcees probably should.

"So, how are you?" Mark asked.

"Great! Almost all set. Lily and I are very excited about our trip."

Mark squirmed.

"I'm not exactly thrilled about you taking Lily out of the country, Arabella."

"Please Mark, it's been six months since you last saw Lily. I hardly think us being away makes any difference."

"I've been busy at work Arabella, and Betty…"

"Stop right there! I don't want to hear about Betty. She has nothing to do with Lily."

"You'll understand when you find someone, Belles," Mark added casually.

"Please don't call me that! Right now, our daughter is my main priority. Meeting someone is the last thing on my agenda."

Of course, he completely ignored her request.

"Look Belles, I've found out what a great relationship should be like. What it's like to get the attention we all deserve. A relationship where you actually think about someone else and you don't have to do things on your own."

Arabella almost socked him one.

"Look, you might as well know we are getting engaged as soon as the divorce is finalized," Mark added.

Wow! How's to give a girl a heads up before shooting her in the gut with a cannonball. Arabella suddenly light-headed, surreptitiously grabbed onto the edge of the sofa. All she could think about was Lily. How would her precious child take that piece of news?

Lily appeared in the sitting room. Arabella, not wanting her daughter to see her upset, stood up quickly. "Why don't you take Daddy upstairs and show him what you've packed for our trip?" she encouraged.

Lily looked like she'd rather skin her fluffy toy cat but she reluctantly obeyed her mother.

Mark really hadn't changed, thought Arabella angrily. She wanted him to fight for his daughter, show Lily she still meant the world to him. Arabella felt utterly powerless.

She looked over at Mark's brand-new Hugo Boss jacket. How could he afford this? Some things never change, as he had just thrown it over the chair. She went to move it when she saw his wallet sticking out of the pocket. Rage took over her body and before she knew it, she was rifling through his wallet like a crazed animal. Receipts from restaurants, jewelry shops, and coffee shops sat folded haphazardly. She whipped his cards over, snapping photos of them on her phone. Why she would need pictures of them God alone only knew but she was on a roll and no-one, not even herself could stop her. She unfolded a voucher from a shop in London and removed it.

Serves you right, you tight bastard! Arabella stopped herself. This wasn't good. This wasn't her. This behavior wasn't her. She looked at her hands.

"Night Daddy." Arabella heard Lily upstairs.

Oh crap! She had to put everything back just as she had found it but she couldn't remember the order of things. Arabella shoved all the contents back in and returned the wallet.

She would be an awful spy.

"Lily wants to go to bed, so I'm going to leave you to it. You look like you have everything under control," Mark said.

Under control? Of course things are under control, you nitwit! As they have been for the past eight years. Who did he think was taking care of Lily all this time whilst he went swanning off with Miss Doodah, doing whatever they wanted without a care in the world?

Mark got up to leave, leaning across to kiss Arabella goodnight. Arabella flinched and moved her head away.

"So call me when you land and I will see you both when you get back in three months yeah?" Mark quipped, casually.

"Yes," she said quietly, hoping she would never have to see him again.

Mark left the house where their little family had spent years creating once-in-a-lifetime memories. He didn't so much as look back for a second to even say farewell. He had moved on.

She had to move on too.

The day before their departure, as Arabella packed the rest of their bags, she wondered whether a complete make-over of herself was in order. She had always fancied doing something different with her hair. It seemed so cliché, but now she knew why. It was about change. She reached for the phone.

"Hi, can I book an appointment please? Yes, a color and cut."

Arabella loved this new-found spontaneity, something she could never have had when married to Mark. A decision with Mark would have to be discussed so many times that by the time any decision had been made, Lily would have turned twenty-one. He was the CEO of procrastinating.

Arabella arrived at the hairdresser's ready for a change. This is what her book called the "knock 'em dead stage."

She had moved through the "pissed off stage" and the "I want to chop off his balls stage" and was nearly at the "FU stage." She was looking forward to that.

Arabella arrived home and took a photo of her new look. She felt younger, freer. She looked a bit like Cameron Diaz. It helped make her feel like she was ready for the new changes in her life. She sent it to the girls, with the message. *The house is sorted, and so am I.*

Arabella surveyed her work. The house was all packed up, and the suitcases were lined up in the corner waiting to be removed. She was ready to start her new life. Arabella received a text from the girls.

We are all coming over to say goodbye.

PART TWO TITANIC

Jack: "Where to, Miss?"
Rose: "To the stars."

Arabella hated flying. In fact, she hated it so much she wondered whether she should just scrap the entire trip. She didn't want to worry Lily in the airport, so she spent the entire time grinning like a Cheshire cat on crack. Her cheeks ached so much she very much hoped her mouth would eventually spring back to normal.

Oddly, flying had never been a problem in the past. Arabella used to enjoy those rare moments of quiet sitting on the plane, away from everything, giving her the opportunity to read. But after the trip to New York a few years earlier, well, let's just say she would never be the same again. Their flight had taken off from Heathrow airport, Arabella and Lily were still making eyes at the gurgling baby in the seat in front. Suddenly turbulence hit the plane with such a force, it lasted for about twenty minutes. Passengers were screaming and crying, convinced they would crash at any moment.

Arabella, snapping into survival mode, turned to Lily, hugged her tightly and reassured her everything would be okay and that she wouldn't let anything happen to her. With fear rip-roaring through her whole body and unconvinced by her own diatribe, she calmly attempted to distract her daughter with stories and food. When the turbulence finally died down, Lily, seemingly unaffected, smiled and went back to watching her movie. Arabella, on the other hand, turned into a nervous wreck. Her body, reacting violently, started to shake and she couldn't stop crying. Eventually six hours later, trapped in her own version of hell, the women next to her handed her a sleeping tablet. Arabella knocked it back without a second thought and only woke up as they landed in New York.

She hadn't even given that flight a second thought until the next time she was on a plane about to take off. Suddenly out of nowhere, she started freaking out. Sweat poured from her body and she couldn't breathe. A steward rushed to get an oxygen canister and she sat attached to it for hours. It was mortifying! Lily, trying not to make a fuss, continued watching her movie whilst Arabella continued to hyperventilate. To make matters worse, the stewards were all about seventy years old and clearly unable to help any of the passengers should the plane go down. Arabella, now absolutely paranoid about flight safety, watched as the steward took the canister back, but was convinced she hadn't turned it off properly. She had read somewhere that the valve must be turned clockwise all the way otherwise it might explode, so Arabella spent the entire flight watching the cupboard, terrified it might do just that. Every time she got off the plane after a flight she looked like she had gone ten rounds with Mike Tyson. Arabella tried to push any negative thoughts out of her mind. This was an important trip, there was no backing out now.

They called their seat number and Arabella began her routine, kissing and blessing the plane as she walked on. She counted the number of rows to the closest exits, recalling a program about plane crashes from months back that highlighted the fact that most people die fumbling in the dark because they can't find the exits. She practiced undoing her seatbelt, not once but several times, preparing herself in case trouble hit. She knew she looked like a mad woman and although she felt like one, she didn't care. Their lives were at stake, dammit!

She bent down and checked for the life jacket under her seat, making sure it was easy to access. She informed the staff on duty of her fears and possible panic attacks and made sure she could check in with the pilot if need be. She read and re-read the safety manual several times and then tapped her head three times continually, as if she was touching wood. She squeezed onto Lily's arm with her left hand and with her right held onto her necklace, attached to her wedding and engagement ring, her good luck charm. Hmmm, perhaps she needed to rethink that part of her safety routine, she thought to herself. As soon as she was able, she ordered a glass of champagne and threw it back like a woman possessed. Okay, she was ready to begin their journey.

Lily was just as excited as Arabella when Los Angeles came into view.

"Mummy look! It's from your favorite show *Entourage*."

Arabella imagined herself being greeted by Ari Gold, waiting at the bottom of the steps to meet her.

"Today and only today I'm gonna open my doors like Ellis fucking Island!"

"I know darling, I can see," was all she managed to say as a flood of joy passed through her.

Lily grabbed her hand and whispered to her mum, "We're at our new home Mummy."

Lily was right. Arabella felt like she was home too. A sanctuary away from drama, away from divorce.

They entered customs and waited in a long queue. Arabella told Lily not to say anything but to look tired so they could pass through quickly. And it worked! A kindly customs officer invited them to skip the line and before she knew it they were officially in LaLa land.

"I love this place already," Arabella grinned.

Arabella just about managed to lift their five suitcases off the belt when an officer came out of nowhere and said, "Excuse me ma'am, but could you come with us please?"

Arabella, a little taken aback, nodded her head as they were ushered into a little room.

"We just have a few questions for you, ma'am."

Oh dear God they were going to be arrested. This was it! She and Lily would be deported and that would be the end of their American dream. No, no, no. She wouldn't survive another twelve hours on a plane. Perhaps prison wasn't such a bad place after all. I mean, she could rock an orange jump suit. And who cares about prison food? She didn't eat much anyway. But Lily... her poor precious Lily...

"Ma'am what are your plans whilst you're here?" the officer enquired sternly.

Arabella thought carefully for a moment before answering. Should she tell him all about last Christmas? Mark, Betty, the whole lot? And how she needed to get as far away from them as possible? No, she decided against it. He did look rather scary with his big beard and gun attached to his hip.

She could grab Lily and make a run for it but what if ten guards broke the door down and jumped on top of her, wrenching Lily from her arms, kicking and screaming? Her cries would attract hundreds of people, turning it into a massive brawl as they tried to get her daughter back. Nope, she would keep it simple.

"I think we'll go to Starbucks," she said.

The officer looked at her as if he hadn't quite heard her correctly. Arabella, like a gazelle about to be eaten by a pack of rabid dogs, could only stare back at him, rooted to the spot, too panicked to move a muscle.

Silence.

And then miraculously, the officer stamped their papers and let them go. Arabella could have kissed him.

"WELCOME TO AMERICA!!!"

Arabella and Lily took a taxi along the coast, to the place they planned on renting for the immediate future. She had found a little one bedroom that was much cheaper than the endless holiday rentals on offer. They didn't have to sign a long-term contract, thus were free to move on whenever their hearts desired which suited Arabella just perfectly.

They pulled up outside what appeared to be an old beach cottage that hadn't been updated in years, with a little terrace out front. It was minuscule to be fair, but it had an open plan kitchen with an adorable sitting room alongside, Arabella fell in love with it. She almost guffawed at the thought of what her mother's face would look like if she saw what they were moving into. The entire cottage including the bathroom could fit into her mother's dressing room and that was not an understatement. But Arabella didn't care what anyone else thought. She was elated! This was hers and Lily's. All theirs! She could smell the ocean from the terrace. A smell that Arabella would soon associate with home. They unloaded their suitcases, bright-eyed and bushy tailed despite the vast time difference and hours they spent traveling. They both were eager to explore their new surroundings but it was getting dark; adventures would have to wait till later.

"Brush your teeth darling, and I will make our beds up."

Arabella pulled out clothes and blankets and Lily's favorite soft toy, a little piglet, and made a comfortable bed for them all on the floor.

Lily and Arabella snuggled, holding each other close. She would never forget that night as long as she lived. She had done it. She had brought them half way across the world. And this was just the beginning…

Bridget "I choose vodka and Chakka Khan."

The next few days were a bit of a blur for Arabella as she tried to gather her bearings and make her way around a foreign city. Keeping her eco-friendly lifestyle in mind, and not wanting to buy anything new, she began trawling the second-hand shops and antique marts. She didn't want to get too much either, as she would have to leave it all behind when she went back in three months. But she did want Lily to feel like she had a proper home whilst they were there. Arabella felt like a kid in a candy store, free to pick whatever she wished. She was in heaven.

By the end of the first week, their little home looked almost habitable. Arabella purchased a daybed and set it up in the sitting room whilst Lily settled in the little bedroom. Lily's toys found a home in a chest of drawers Arabella secured and cutlery and crockery were put away in the kitchen. They had great fun searching for odds and ends in various stores. Arabella attempted to buy fairy lights but apparently in LA no-one knew what she meant when she asked any of the salespeople. They all looked at her as though she was speaking Mandarin.

"Ah, you must mean Christmas lights!" a young assistant said.

"I suppose I do," she answered. Arabella practically glowed.

If only they knew how much she loved these pretty lights. She would happily string Christmas lights all over their new home no matter what time of year it was.

"Mummy I've run out of underwear," Lily shouted.

Arabella dreaded going to the Laundromat. She walked past it several times but didn't dare venture in. She had no idea where to start. It looked like big scary monsters ready to devour her.

"Ok, no time like the present. Get all your dirty clothes together," Arabella quipped.

This should be fun, she thought sarcastically. She held onto the notion that the whole experience would be exactly like one of those Levi's commercials. A tall, gorgeous hunk with a solid tanned body ripped with muscles would walk in and strip in front of her. He would tear her clothes off and makes wild passionate love to her on the dryer.

Okay, first of all, she needed to get out more and second of all, maybe she should leave Lily at home. She hoped the Laundromat might be the code word for "Let's get it on!" A place where no kids should ever set foot. Arabella searched inside, hoping to protect her daughter from any random gorgeous half-naked men but alas, only the washing machines and dryers stared back at her. Never having been into a Laundromat before Arabella felt somewhat traumatized.

What goes where? They all look the same to me, she thought.

"It's easy mummy. We just put the clothes in here," Lily said as she found a washing machine.

"Yes of course."

Oh dear Lord, she felt silly. This wasn't a dream whereby she was forced into taking a calculus exam, and two hours later she was still trying to figure out the meaning of the word "calculus." No, she could figure this out. Arabella should purchase Lily a Supergirl outfit and she could be her side kick. I mean, her daughter was seriously bad ass. Nothing seemed to faze her. They made a perfect team. Arabella was unsure whether they could leave their clothes and come back, so the two of them watched their belongings circle the machine for the entire cycle. Clothing, clean! Arabella could tick another item off their list.

Over the next few days, they drove around exploring the beach and other famous tourist destinations. School in the UK had agreed to Lily taking the time off, only if she were to keep up with all her school work. It was imperative that Arabella found her a tutor as soon as possible. As they sat in their local Starbucks contemplating what to do for the rest of their day, a man walked over and started talking to them. Arabella loved that Americans were bold enough to speak to whomever in public places. The British were far more reserved and it warmed Arabella's cockles that she could interact so freely.

"Oh my God, I love your accent, where are you from?" the man asked, interested.

"London," she replied with a smile.

"Do you know the queen?"

Arabella, who just at that moment decided to take a sip of her English tea, almost spat it out, unable to contain the fit of giggles about to overtake her. Surely he wasn't serious? The man waited patiently for an answer and Arabella realized that yes, he was.

"Uh, well, not personally no." She almost laughed again, when she saw the disappointment on his face.

"You know your daughter has a great look. Is she an actress?" he continued.

"I'm Audrey Hepburn," Lily replied with a conviction that baffled her own mother. Lily elevated her chin, turning to show the man her perfect profile, without breaking character.

"No, she used to do ballet, but that was about it," Arabella responded.

"Well I'm casting for an upcoming film and I would love your daughter to come to the audition if she's available." the man said.

Arabella thought about their day sashaying around town, and pretended to check her schedule.

"I think we can fit it in," she said.

"Great, here's my email. Contact me and I will send you the details."

After he walked off, Lily told her mother in great detail how one day she would be winning an Oscar. Arabella had no idea where Lily got her incredibly vivid imagination from.

Okay, maybe she did.

Lily held on to her phone as if it were a microphone, practicing her speech.

"I would like to thank my Mummy for everything she's done for me. If she never moved us over to LA for a holiday and hadn't taken me to that Starbucks on that fateful day we would never have met Steven Spielberg."

How Lily managed to perfect her American accent Arabella had no idea.

Life in LA was turning out to be better than Arabella could've ever imagined. She instantly thought about messaging Mark as she wanted to share with him the great news. But before their departure, he made it perfectly clear he wasn't to be disturbed whilst he was away on holiday with Betty. After the initial split, Arabella found it extremely difficult not to message Mark regarding everyday life. They spent ten years calling and texting each other countless times a day so stopping cold turkey was not as easy as you might think. Sometimes her fingers had a mind of their own and would just begin texting Mark after a significant event had occurred and before she could stop herself, she had sent them without thinking. She chastised herself relentlessly after she had behaved so stupidly, but almost a year after the affair she had mastered the art of restraint.

Arabella found messaging one of her friends helped to cure the need to text her ex-husband. Charlotte, a neighbor whom Arabella had recently met, offered her friendship wholeheartedly.

They went walking along the beach footpath and had become confidantes in a very short period of time. The fresh air and the sunshine filled this small beach resort with happiness from all the locals. It was just outside the centre of LA, not far from the metro. It was a little safe haven that they had found. Charlotte, a divorcee, had a boy a bit older than Lily, and they also become friends immediately. He even taught Arabella how to skateboard.

Arabella picked up the phone and called her friend.

"Hi, Charlotte here," she had said in a southern drawl.

"Hi, It's Arabella."

Arabella filled her in on the day's events.

"Wow, that's awesome! You must be so proud and pleased."

Arabella knew Charlotte would be supportive.

"I am, but I'm a tad nervous," Arabella confessed.

"Don't be, it's a fab thing to do. I should know."

Charlotte was once a child star and re-runs of her show still played. She and her son lived off her royalty cheques. Arabella found this rather interesting.

That night Arabella watched Lily sleeping, snuggled up to piglet and hoped and prayed that the entertainment industry was the move for Lily. Kevin, the man they had met, sent Arabella the details for the audition and Lily was expected to recite lines from a script the next day, which seemed simple enough. Lily seemed happy at the thought of auditioning, unlike her mother, who was filled with fear.

The next day, they pulled up to a tatty looking building with "Casting" emblazoned out front. *This must be the place*, Arabella thought, as about twenty other little girls were being ushered in by their parents. Some of the children looked far from happy with the prospect of what was about to occur and others were grinning from ear to ear. Arabella heard one of the mother's coaxing her daughter.

"If you go in, I'll give you $200," she urged.

"But I don't want to," the little girl wailed.

"If you don't go, there will be no birthday party for you this year!" the mother snapped.

The little girl, now traumatized, burst into tears.

"Great, now your face is all red! Look what you've done.

You've messed everything up!" The angry mother practically dragged her daughter to their car.

Arabella was horrified.

"If I ever get like that mother, shoot me, please," Arabella said to Lily.

Lily giggled.

"You need to sign in," a sweet looking woman told Arabella.

"Oh thank you. It's our first time here, we've never done this before."

A silence came over the room. She was obviously not supposed to admit that out loud. Arabella signed the sheet and then waited. Each little girl went in and came out in a matter of minutes. Arabella shook her head. She drove miles to get here, for what, two minutes? She must be crazy!

A rather stern looking woman came out of the room and looked around.

"Lily," she called out.

Arabella gave Lily a reassuring hug.

"Have fun darling. You're going to be great!" Arabella felt disapproving stares once more from a few of the mothers but shrugged it off. *What on earth am I supposed to say?* she wondered.

After about ten minutes Lily came out beaming.

"I got it, mummy! I got it!"

Arabella froze. She wasn't quite sure what was happening. She began chuckling nervously and for some reason couldn't stop. "Oh sweetie, I know you want it but you couldn't have. These girls have all been doing it a lot longer. Next time maybe, okay?" she said as she grabbed Lily and took her outside.

"Tell me what happened," Arabella said.

"Well, Kevin was really nice. He thought I did a really good job and then he asked me if I would like to do it."

Arabella looked at her daughter sympathetically.

"Oh my darling, that doesn't mean you have the job. But I'm so proud of you! Come on let's go and get a Pinkberry. I saw one just around the corner."

Lily immediately forgot about the audition and bounded over to Pinkberry with Arabella hot on her heels. Lily adored Pinkberry. It was the trendy frozen yoghurt place everyone went to. You could help yourself to as much as you wanted but only Arabella knew you paid by the weight and always tried to steer Lily towards the smallest container. She had found this out the hard way on their first visit there, when they ended up with a fifteen-dollar yoghurt! She was a single mother now, so being frugal was a necessity.

They sat outside guzzling the pear flavored yogurt with chocolate bits and strawberries. It was exquisite! Arabella's phone rang and she fumbled around in her bag, eventually finding it.

"Hello, Arabella speaking," she said, her mouth full of chocolate.

"Hi Arabella, it's Kevin. We love Lily and the producer wants to call her back in today. Any chance you could pop back in about an hour?"

Arabella was stunned.

Lily was right.

"Of course."

"Great."

Before Arabella could ask any more questions, Kevin was gone.

"Okay, well you obviously made an impression my darling," she turned to Lily. "The nice people at the studio want to see you again."

Lily smiled knowingly. "I told you I had it. I am Audrey Hepburn Mummy. I really am."

"Yes you are, my darling. Yes you are." Arabella agreed.

Back at the studio, Arabella was a wreck. She wondered how the other mothers did this without blowing a gasket at some point. You'd think Arabella herself was in there auditioning.

Arabella thought it best to distract herself and attempted to start a conversation with one of the mothers. What a stupid idea that was.

"So, has your daughter done this before?" she smiled at the nearest woman.

The woman looked at Arabella with an air of superiority and began to list prime time shows that her daughter had starred in. *This must be one of those serious showbiz moms*, Arabella thought. The mother looked like a fire-breathing dragon who was about to swallow Arabella whole, leaving her bones for Lily to find when she came out. Her poor daughter would be traumatized for life.

"Yours?" she said dismissively.

"Um no, this is our first audition," Arabella mumbled, feeling a little silly for engaging in conversation.

The mothers kept staring at Arabella like there was a big secret they all knew about and she didn't. Arabella, feeling uncomfortable, pretended to distract herself by looking busy on her phone. Then suddenly she had an idea. What if she began detailing notes about her experiences here in LA and perhaps start a blog? She hadn't written much recently, so it was the perfect opportunity to start again. It would give her something to do and she might enjoy it. Not that anyone would read it, she thought, but it was worth a try.

The children eventually came out, looking equally happy and exhausted. Arabella on the other hand, was so bored she couldn't wait to get out of the room. It felt like a pressure cooker about to blow its lid, the tension was so intense.

"Thank you for leaving your children with us, we will let you know," the PA said and departed to another room.

"Okay darling, let's go."

"Oh Mummy, can we do it again? It was such fun." Lily shrieked.

Arabella knew if she was to stay sane in this situation again, she would need to be prepared and bring a book, some paper or a knife. Anything!

Arabella led Lily out to the car.

"Can't we have another Pinkberry Mummy?" Lily begged.

"No my darling, just because we ate one today doesn't mean it happens every time, it was a treat."

Lily, crestfallen, accepted her mum's decision and hopped in the car, ready to go home.

A few days passed and since Arabella hadn't heard from Kevin, she assumed they had given the part to one of the more experienced girls. She took Lily to a painting class at the Getty Centre, where they tried their hand at another creative endeavor. Arabella went to the restroom to check her voice mails on their break, hoping to hear about a tutor for Lily.

"Hi Arabella, it's Kevin here. We want to see Lily again, not for the original role that we saw her for, but another one. The producers loved her and we think she has great potential."

Arabella was dumbfounded. She let out a squeak.

"We will give you all the details soon. This is my office number, if you have any questions just let me know. She will need to get a work permit, the studio said they would sort that out. You will then be provided with a chaperone visa as she is underage. The visa lasts for three years so be prepared to stay around. Lily will do well here!"

Arabella, ready to jump up and down with glee, remained calm as she needed to discuss the matter with Mark first. The last thing she wanted to do was get Lily's hopes up unnecessarily.

She immediately called her mother.

"She got it!" Arabella yelled.

"Aaaahhhhhhhhh! I knew she would, my darling! She is so amazingly talented. She takes after her Sou Sou. So when does she start?"

"Mom, it's not as simple as that. It means we need to stay here for longer and I need to check with Mark first before making any decisions."

"Darling, darling. There is nothing to think about. This is an incredible opportunity for Lily and who knows, you may even meet a gorgeous director and marry him," she replied cheekily.

Oh for goodness sake! Did her entire family live in cloud cuckoo land? Obviously, as immediately Arabella saw herself walking down the aisle in a wedding dress...

The wedding party laughed.

"I was totally smitten the moment she brought her daughter on set and shouted at me for not providing her with warm clothing. We were shooting in winter, you see..."

"Mum, seriously? I'm not even divorced yet."

"Speaking of the divorce, my darling, another letter from the lawyers came today. It looks like Mark has completed everything on his end financially and so if you agree then the divorce should be finalized soon."

Arabella went silent, trying to catch her breath. She knew it was inevitable, she was prepared for it, so why did it still hurt like hell?

"Are you there darling?" her mum asked, concerned.

"Yes, mum. Okay, thanks for letting me know," Arabella hung up, willing herself not to cry.

It's the final stretch, Arabella. You will get through this, she encouraged herself.

SOMETHING ABOUT MARY

Mary: "Who needs him? I've got a vibrator."

"The divorce should be finalized soon."

Her mother's words rang through her head. Arabella sat on her deck listening to the waves, troubled by the fact that though she believed she had moved on by now, thoughts about Mark still lingered. Of course they would, they spent nearly ten years together.

Did he ever think about what they had? Or were she and Lily already a distant memory? God, how she wanted to just move on unencumbered by memories of him, least of all the good ones.

She remembered the time she went on holiday with Lily and a friend. They were lying by the pool, eyes closed, soaking in the scorching heat, when all of a sudden Arabella felt someone standing over her. She opened her eyes to see Mark staring at her with so much love that she leapt into his arms, kissing him all over.

"Surprise!" was all he could say, equally happy to see her. It was so romantic. He then very annoyingly stayed for the rest of the week, expecting to be looked after and fed.

Actually, that wasn't a good example.

There was the time he arranged a surprise birthday party for her. Well actually, now that she recalled, Arabella knew about it beforehand and ended up doing most of the preparations. Again, not a great example. Come to think of it, Mark was not at all considerate or romantic and had a history of forgetting many birthdays, anniversaries and special occasions. *Betty, you are welcome to him.*

She put Lily to bed and enjoyed a glass of crisp white wine out on her small terrace. Arabella truly treasured these moments. She could hear the waves and feel the warm sun on her skin. It was magical. A far cry from the English cold. Arabella perused her surroundings, appreciating what she had achieved in the limited space. Fairy lights decorated the railings, a couple of squashy bean bags and a mini heater completed the area. Cushioning her face in her hands against her sun-kissed skin she felt an unfamiliar bump on her cheek.

"Oh my God, it's a spot. A massive, painful spot!"

When was the last time she'd had a spot? *Please don't let my body get savaged by a boat load of spots!* It's not like she was going on a date anytime soon, but now that she was getting divorced a girl had to be prepared for the inevitable.

Arabella's emails beeped. Oh crap! It was a notification from Finder, the online dating application the girls made her download weeks back. Setting it up had completely slipped her mind. Maybe it was time to take a peek. She was curious to see who was around.

She hoped no one could see what she was doing. Okay, swipe right for yes and left for no. Left, left, left. Hmmm, okay, right, left, right, oh crap I meant left!

PING!

Oh boy. Arabella panicked.

You matched, continue playing?

Arabella was intrigued. She saw a message appear.

I don't want to beat around the bush unless it's your bush. Can we have sex tonight?

Urgh! Arabella was mortified. She quickly put down the phone as if being watched. I suppose it was quite flattering, she thought. He wasn't bad looking and he obviously fancied her.

Oh God, am I now so desperate I'm considering going out with a man whose opening line includes the word "bush?

Arabella tinkered with the app, trying to figure out how it all worked. It was so clever it actually told you who was nearby! Swipe left, swipe left, swipe left, *Okay. You're cute and local. Swipe right.*

A text pinged in her Inbox.

"Nice to meet you, you're beautiful." Bryan.

"*Thank you.*" Arabella wrote, pleased with the compliment.

"Want to hook up?" Bryan was clearly in a bit of a rush.

"How many weirdos were on this site?" Arabella was not in the mood.

She was trying very hard not to be a prude but did these men not want to have a conversation before having sex? She had obviously been out of the loop for way too long. She finished her wine and made her way inside to go to bed. Bryan would have to wait until tomorrow if he was still keen.

Arabella awoke the next morning to dozens of red notifications on her phone, all from Bryan. He was a persistent bugger and proceeded to text her all day. Eventually, Arabella gave in and said yes to a drink that evening.

"Sounds great, see you later." he said.

Arabella hadn't been on a date for years. Shaving was probably a good idea as she had never heard a man say they loved hairy legs.

A pedicure might also go a long way as she always had filthy feet from wearing flip flops. She heard her mother's voice echoing in her head:

"Don't go off with strangers, but if you do make sure you look good."

Okay, so looking good, check. The "don't go off with strangers" part... well, she had spoken to Bryan on the phone. Technically he was no longer a stranger, right?

What if she was taken hostage, kept in the basement and used as a sex slave? Her beautiful daughter would be motherless and Arabella would be trapped, forced to do awful things for the next twenty years. Eventually, when she did escape by hitting her captor over the head with a table leg that she'd sawn off with the end of her toothbrush, Lily would be a mother of two gorgeous children, her name in lights wherever she went.

Maybe meeting him was not such a great plan after all. She messaged him.

"What do you do, exactly?" she enquired.

Seemed like a good place to start.

"I'm an engineer."

Uh okay, what would she have in common with an engineer, she thought. After Mark moved out, Arabella made a list of attributes she would want her next man to have.

They were as follows:

Creative

Tall

Dark

Handsome

Able to write poetry.

Must sing.

The list seemed pretty weak now and she was still adding attributes to her list as she went along, but as finding a man was not currently a priority, she hadn't quite finished. Her list was starting to look slightly different as she realized she didn't really need a man at the moment at all. Maybe just a drink and a stolen kiss would suffice.

Arabella picked up her phone. She had emailed Mark about Lily's job offer the day she received the details. Surprise, surprise – she was still waiting for a response. Did he not realize time was of the essence?

Another message from Bryan came through as she was checking her emails.

"Don't plan to go home tonight."

Yes, Arabella still had a lot to learn about the dating world but this man was creepy, right? How did the conversation go from I'm an engineer to let's have sex? He didn't even have enough class to pretend he was interested in getting to know her.

It reminded her of the time, not long after Mark had left, when she was invited to a party. Alice insisted she got her arse out of bed and got out into the real world. Although she literally couldn't think of anything worse, she bought a new dress, jumped in a taxi and made her way to the party.

It was a black-tie event, held at the Canadian embassy, where Royalty and a ton of celebrities would be in attendance. She loved getting dressed up and looked forward to forgetting about her disaster of a marriage for one night. Jen ran up to her as soon as she arrived and introduced her to anyone they came into contact with.

"This is Arabella, she's getting divorced and is a single mum."

Thrilling introduction, she thought. *Is there a gas oven anywhere in the vicinity so I can stick my head in it?*

"This is Patrick, he's loaded."

Well, her night was certainly looking up, she mused.

Arabella, nervous about meeting new people, knocked back a couple of glasses of champagne. She felt relaxed and was about to walk up the grand staircase when she spotted a dark, handsome man. She pictured herself in that scene from the *Thomas Crown Affair* where she is Rene Russo and the man is Pierce Brosnan, aka Mr. Crown. The lights would dim, the music would start, and he would grab her, dancing back and forth with her in the light. Her dress would be sheer and they focus only on each other. He would take her home and they would make love on the stairs, alongside a massive sculpture of two entwined lovers. He would pour champagne all over her.

The words "Hello, I'm James" abruptly interrupted her daydream.

God, he's gorgeous and could give Pierce Brosnan a run for his money, Arabella thought.

"Hi, I'm Arabella," she said weakly, hoping she wasn't making goo goo eyes at him.

"Would you like to go for a walk?" he asked.

A walk? Was that code for something? Maybe for "I want to rip all your clothes off and take you here, right now".

"A walk?"

"You do know how to walk I take it?"

Arabella, flummoxed, managed a weak smile. *Focus Arabella, you're going to blow it.*

James put his arm through hers and led her outside. "You must see the pool," he said.

"Okay." She would see anything with him.

James led her towards a magnificent pool, surrounded by marble statues. Amber lights flickered whilst a string quartet played in the background.

"So you're Jen's friend?" he enquired.

"Yes," was all she managed to say. She really was monstrously unprepared for an encounter with such a hottie. What does a newly single mummy say? She tried racking her brains for something, anything to talk about.

"Well if I tell you a secret can you promise you'll keep it?" he whispered in her ear.

A rush of adrenaline surged through her body. God this man had an overwhelming effect on her.

"Of course." Arabella willed him to go on. His face was inches from hers and she could feel his hot breath, tickle her skin.

"I've been watching you since you arrived and I have a proposition for you."

Arabella was elated. *He wants me. Oh my God, this hunk of a man wants me! We need to leave now. But where will we go?* Arabella's body, now on fire, knew if he undressed her and took her right here in the open, she would let him. She was so horny she could scream!

"I would like you to be my mistress." He said it like he was handing her the key to Golden Gate Bridge.

Uh, excuse me? Was this man on drugs?

Arabella, reeling from shock, couldn't manage to utter an actual word.

"I'm getting married in a couple of weeks but I need a mistress. You won't be seen in public with me but you will accompany me to all my events. I will pay for everything you need and you will be there for me afterwards, you will never want for anything."

Arabella stared at him blankly, still unable to speak. Looking around for the joke to be revealed.

"I will leave you to think about it."

James walked back into the building and Arabella thought she was the one who had unknowingly taken drugs that evening. Or perhaps she should take drugs in order to better understand what had actually just happened.

She started to replay the scene over in her head. Could she even consider such a thing? As usual, her mind disappeared off towards her favourite place, her fantasy land. If she said yes, she could flesh out her own terms and conditions. She would need a private jet, an allowance, a car, a book deal, a house in the South of France, a flat in London. Why stop there when she could also have a flat in New York?

Oh dear, what was she thinking? Of course, she couldn't have an affair with another woman's husband. She might as well call herself

Betty and be done with it. No! How dare he anyway? What was he going to do? Leave some money on the bed as he left each night?

"Arabella." It was Jen. "I thought you'd left, are you having a nice time?"

"Yes thank you, it's wonderful," she lied. "But I think I'm going to head home now. I'm quite tired."

"Of course, message me tomorrow."

"Okay, love you."

Arabella didn't go back inside to address James. She never wanted to see him again.

Romeo: "Did my heart love till now? Forswear it sight for I ne'er saw true beauty till this night."

Arabella decided to forget about all men, including Bryan, as she hardly needed the complication. Her phone rang.

"Hi Arabella, it's Kevin."

"Hi, Kevin, good to hear from you."

"So, everything is looking good. Moving forward, we think it would help Lily tremendously if you could find her an acting coach."

This was all new to Arabella. Acting coaches, headshots, agents. She hoped it wouldn't cost an arm and a leg but she supposed you needed to spend money in order to make money.

The next day Arabella followed his instruction and Lily was delighted at the prospect of getting an acting teacher. Lily was preparing to change her name to Audrey Lily Hepburn. She planned all the films and TV shows that she would star in, and was already deciding what she was going to buy with the money that she would earn.

As Arabella was following directions on Google maps in Beverly Hills, she zoned out from what Lily was saying and instead imagined herself living in one of the mansions. Maybe she would end up married to a plastic surgeon, which could turn out to be very useful. Then she would be neighbors with the Kardashians, inviting everyone over for tea. They would praise her English tea making skills.

Arabella and Lily arrived at their final destination, at one of the more modest houses on the street. It was still incredibly beautiful, almost British like, with wisteria hanging over its front door.

She noticed another mother waiting outside.

"Is he any good?" she asked.

"The best in the business," the woman answered. Arabella was relieved.

The door opened and the hottest of hot men stood staring back at her, a mixture of Daniel Craig and Brad Pitt. Arabella actually went weak at the knees and everything appeared to slow down around her.

"Hi, I'm Tommy."

Arabella barely heard the words coming out of his mouth.

"I'm Arabella and this is Lily," she croaked.

I'm divorced, single, free and available. She hoped he couldn't read her mind.

"We are here for a session, I mean here for a good going over. I mean, I need you to look at me, my daughter, Lily…"

Oh dear God what was happening to her? She couldn't string a bloody sentence together.

"Uh, we are here for you to look at Lily's speech," she finally got out.

Arabella went bright red and sat down. The other mother smiled knowingly as she walked away.

Terrific Tommy smiled dreamily, looking down at Arabella's toes.

"Nice feet," he winked.

Arabella's heart turned to jelly as Lily went inside. *Am I supposed to leave now,* Arabella wondered? *But I want to go in with you, tantalizing Tommy. Can you help me with my audition? Tom, Tommy? Get a grip Arabella, there are kids around! Not to mention your sweet, little daughter.*

Her heart skipped a beat and she floated back to her car, breathing heavily.

Okay, calm down! You have half an hour before you lay your eyes on lover boy again. Go and get the cash out to pay him and grab your lunch. Must not think about Tommy, must not think about Tommy! She grinned like a fool as she pulled up to the cash point. Only in America could you get everything you needed without ever leaving your car. The ATM, Starbucks, the launderette… practically everything had a drive through. She popped her card into the machine, it beeped.

"Unable to proceed with transaction."

Arabella was stumped. Huh? She was due her money from Mark today, she should have plenty. She clicked on 'balance.' The machine was right. There was nothing in her account. What the hell was Mark playing at? Did he think Lily lived on money that grew on trees? It wasn't rocket science. Maintenance was to be paid at the beginning of each month. Crap, what was she going to do? She hated having to ask for money. Arabella couldn't wait for the day when she could tell him she didn't need anything from him anymore.

Her goal, more than anything, was to be financially independent. Not having a working visa meant she couldn't work, which was not ideal and also far from aided her long-term vision. The proceeds from the house were for her rainy-day fund and she tried to live off the allowance she was given. They just about got by as long as Mark's money came in on time. Another example of Mark's selfishness was when Lily needed braces desperately and he said no. Mark said if she needed them so badly, she could pay with her new earnings if she was going to end up acting. Arabella was furious! He didn't want her to start in the industry in the first place, but was now expecting her to support herself aged nine?

Arabella raged. She called Mark's number.

"Hello," Mark yelled.

Arabella could hear club music playing in the background. Where was he?

"Hi Mark, it's Arabella," she said annoyed.

Silence. Of course he wasn't going to make this easy for her.

"I'm afraid the money hasn't come through yet and there are things Lily needs today."

She waited for the barrage of excuses.

"I don't have enough money, I haven't paid myself yet. I will try and get it to you tomorrow," he whined.

Arabella knew this was a lie because she had seen all his statements from the financial disclosure report. Mark was doing just fine. Arabella tried to keep calm.

"Mark, I need our money today please. I have to pay for Lily's things."

Again, silence.

"Give me five minutes."

The phone went dead. She sat in the car park, waiting. Arabella's thoughts drifted to a dark and lonely place. She could get through this. She must not lose faith! Arabella encouraged herself. The day Arabella could support herself and not rely on Mark could not come soon enough. He enjoyed having this financial control over her.

Her thoughts were broken by a ping.

"*It's done.*"

Arabella went to the ATM and withdrew $200. Phew!

She pulled back round to Tommy's just in time.

"Lily was great! Real potential, just like her mom." The man was definitely flirting with her. "So what do you do?"

She didn't want to say she was just a mum. I mean, how boring. But she also didn't want to make something up. She wanted to sound intelligent, interesting. Luckily Lily stepped in.

"Mummy writes," she said proudly.

"Oh yes, I write. Up all hours writing," Arabella added.

"You don't look like you're up all hours."

The man was incorrigible, but she liked it.

Arabella blushed furiously. She paid him the money and told Lily to get into the car.

"If you need me again, let me know," he said affectionately.

Arabella could feel his eyes bore into her as she walked back to the car. She turned, half-expecting him to follow her, but alas he didn't. She got in the car, Lily was smirking.

"You like him Mummy, don't you?" she said happily.

Arabella didn't say a word. She didn't have to. Her face said it all.

****

Lily and Arabella were enjoying a morning walk. A few days had passed since Lily's lesson and Arabella felt they were finally getting into the swing of things when her phone rang. It was Mark. He didn't beat around the bush.

"There's something I need to tell you."

Silence.

Okay, get to it Mark. He really did have the flair for the dramatics.

"Betty is pregnant."

What? She knew Mark wanted more children, which had been one of their burning issues. They had tried a number of times but it didn't work. She told him the universe was making the decision for them as Arabella knew at the time they couldn't afford it, but it didn't deter them.

What did he expect her to say? Arabella put the phone down, her body motionless. Lily was talking but all Arabella heard was white noise.

Betty is pregnant.

"Mummy stop!" Lily screamed.

Arabella jerked into focus as a car came to a complete stop within inches of her on the road, slamming its brakes. Thank God Lily was trailing behind her.

"Are you OK?" Arabella checked on her daughter.

"Yes Mummy, why weren't you looking?" Lily asked

concerned.

"I was my darling, I was."

How was Lily going to cope with this news? A new sibling?

Arabella sat down on the side of the road and hugged Lily. That was too close a call. What was she thinking? What if something had happened to Lily? Arabella considered her options. Perhaps it was time for them to speak to someone, to help Lily through this next emotional upheaval. Maybe this was too important for Arabella to try and help Lily deal with by herself. Lily had had to deal with a separation, then a divorce and now this. Lily was so happy at the moment. She had so many potentially life-changing experiences in front of her. Arabella didn't want this to set her back.

After Lily had gone to bed, shattered by this new news, Arabella spent all evening researching counselors. None of them seemed a good fit. Arabella looked up to the sky and asked the universe to help her and guide her. With no rhyme or reason, a thought came into Arabella's head. What about fairies? Lily loved fairies. She looked up fairies on the internet, not knowing what she would come across. Especially in LA, where one could never be sure what kind of fairies one might find. Would the counselor dress up like a fairy?

Bingo! Arabella found a place called "The Mystic Mountain". They offered sessions to anyone of all ages and one of the ladies was referred to as "Fairy Venus." *Only in LA,* she thought. Arabella called up and booked an appointment immediately. A magical sounding lady answered the phone.

"Welcome to Mystic Mountain, how can we make your day better?"

This was a great idea, Arabella thought. She couldn't wait for tomorrow.

INDECENT PROPOSAL

Diane: "The dress is for sale, I'm not."

Lily couldn't contain herself at the thought of seeing a fairy. Arabella told Lily they were going to a safe place, where she could talk about anything she wanted to. It was her space to be open and just breathe.

"A real fairy, I'm going to meet a real fairy! she gushed. "Should I curtsey, mummy?"

It made Arabella happy to see her daughter so excited.

By the time they got to their appointment, most of the village - including everyone in Starbucks, knew about the visit to the fairy. Lily had told anyone and everyone that she had met that morning.

It was the most magical place. Arabella felt immediately at ease about her decision. Magic Mountain was, in fact, an old house on a narrow vintage street. Incense burned and fairy lights hung from magical looking trees. A mystical feeling of music floated through the air.

"Mummy look at these crystals and these cards and these smelly candles and these necklaces!" Lily wanted to buy it all.

Like Lily, Arabella also appreciated the knick-knacks. They made her feel grounded and at peace.

"Lily?" Arabella turned to see Lily's softly spoken fairy. Arabella thought her daughter would faint from sheer elation.

"Please have her for as much time as you need. She needs to

talk. It's really important," Arabella urged.

"Of course," she fluttered her imaginary wings.

And away Lily went, holding hands with her new best friend.

The staff at the fairy shop fell in love with Lily and looked after her when it was Arabella's turn. Venus sat opposite and proceeded to hold Arabella's hand, breathing and feeling her energy. Arabella, suddenly feeling very emotional, listened intently and let Venus work her magic.

"You must wear more pink, be more girly," Venus said. "Open your heart up, it's okay to let people in," she continued.

"But this isn't about me, it's about Lily, what can I do to help her?" Arabella needed to know. "I want Mark to be happy with someone who could be part of our lives. Part of Lily's at least."

"Give it time, Arabella. I want you to do something for me, this will help Lily to deal with her present emotions."

Venus elaborated and talked about a spell that she wanted Arabella to try.

Arabella returned from her session to a beaming Lily.

"I love my fairy mummy! I must not think bad thoughts and if I do get them I need to learn to let them go. I must also tell you if I'm not feeling happy," Lily gushed, barely taking a breath.

Arabella had given her daughter the same advice on many occasions but of course, she wasn't a fairy.

They jumped back in the car and Arabella announced, "Let's go shopping! I need to buy a watermelon."

Arabella thought deeply about the spell from Venus. She was

aware it seemed a little crazy, but she was willing to try anything to help Lily.

After arriving home that evening, Lily and Arabella made their way to the beach. She stood in the ocean, cold water up to her thighs, holding the watermelon and repeated the incantation Venus had given to her. She had to look like an idiot! Venus told her to offer the watermelon to the sea as a symbolic offering. She threw the watermelon into the ocean and held her daughter tightly whilst simultaneously shouting the spell.

"AARRGGHH!" Arabella screamed. Something was attacking her feet. She crouched down to take a closer look.

Oh no silly me. It's only the watermelon! Arabella laughed at herself. How could she help Lily to move forward with her life when the ocean wouldn't receive the bloody watermelon?

Arabella decided to complete the spell regardless of how ridiculous she thought the whole thing might be. Arabella, still fully dressed, submerged herself in the ocean. Crap! It was freezing. She didn't think she had cleansed the situation but at least she was clean.

Although a hot bath would have been preferable.

She heard Venus's voice.

"Open your mind to what comes to you and Lily."

She closed her eyes and a thought came to her. Salsa dancing! They would try salsa! It was perfect.

"We don't need to tell anyone about the watermelon incident, okay Lily?" Arabella informed her.

"Okay, mummy."

Arabella hoped she hadn't scarred her dear daughter for life.

"Mummies do the strangest things. Good girl."

Once Arabella had dried and warmed up, Lily went to bed. Arabella sat with her laptop on the sofa bed. She googled local dance classes and found one within walking distance. It was run by a committee of ex-salsa dancers that wanted to give back to the community. Arabella, being a perfectionist, couldn't arrive not knowing anything about salsa so she made a plan to book a private lesson first, Lily was bound to pick it up quickly.

Arabella was excited! They could start tomorrow night. Before turning off her emails, she checked one last time for a response from Mark about Lily's next job. Nothing! Arabella had no choice, she would have to make the decision alone. As usual. She knew it was the right move for Lily. Mark had left her to make the decision alone, so that's what she was bloody well going to do. She couldn't wait a day longer, she had a deadline to meet and Mark was fully aware of this.

****

It was the first day of Lily's film shoot. In her enthusiasm, Lily had fed and dressed before Arabella could even open both her eyes that morning. Arabella finally got herself together and they arrived at the studio with plenty of time to kill. After being subjected to a military-like interrogation at the gate and providing more than one type of I.D. they were eventually allowed in.

Customs seemed like a breeze in comparison.

They made their way inside, posters of films lining the long corridors. They waited in a sitting room-style space, no one coming over to offer any help or guidance. Everyone seemed to know each other and they all helped themselves to breakfast whilst catching up on the daily gossip. Arabella and Lily looked at each other, and not wanting to be left out, also grabbed more breakfast and one of the many scripts sitting in a pile.

They were reading Lily's lines when someone came over and informed them the script they were using did not belong to them, but to one of the lead actors. Arabella was told horror stories about the industry. She was also told that you could be fired at the read-through if they didn't like you. They weren't exactly off to a roaring start.

Arabella and Lily were told to head to the read-through and followed everyone else into another room, again laden with food and beverages. With a spread like this, you'd think these people hadn't eaten in years. She laughed as she remembered when she first went to a party in LA and discussed the canapés provided.

"Excuse me, where are the nibbles?" she had asked innocently.

"I'm sorry, the what?" the host looked utterly perplexed.

"Nibbles?" Arabella said slightly less sure of herself. "The food that comes out before the main food?"

A long awkward silence ensued, followed by raucous laughter. Apparently, they were called appetizers here and not nibbles, which had sexual connotations!

Everyone took their seats around a large table in the windowless room and the read-through began. The director and the producers watched the actors like hawks, every so often scribbling pages of notes. Arabella was incredibly anxious, to put it mildly. Lily seemed to be taking it all in her stride. She was so proud of her! Lily's resilience always astounded her. She dealt with every negative situation, including the matter with her father, with absolute grace. She was a force to be reckoned with!

After the read-through Arabella and Lily were told to wait in another windowless room. Arabella was then informed she would be staying in the room all day as parents were "not needed on set". A polite way of saying "NO PARENTS ARE ALLOWED." Luckily she had learnt from the last experience and had come prepared. She began mapping out her blog about a single mum heading to LA. The time whizzed by and she had written a few chapters. Walking in, Lily was grinning from ear to ear and grasping in her little hands a huge sugary chocolate donut.

"I have to go back in ten minutes but first I need the toilet," she said.

Arabella wondered if she planned on relinquishing the donut before relieving herself. Somehow, she didn't think so.

Hours later Lily returned exhausted from the set, having loved the experience. Arabella, on the other hand, had completed almost ten blogs. It had come surprisingly easy to her and she enjoyed it immensely. Maybe someone might be interested in reading them?

As they drove home, Lily fell asleep on the back seat. Arabella looked down at her phone and there was a text from Tommy.

"Fancy a quick drink tonight?"

Arabella perked up. Oh, yes indeed! She could do with getting dressed up and taken out.

"Sure," she messaged back.

Arabella was looking forward to an adult evening with a

handsome, seemingly normal man. Now the real question was, what was she going to wear?

BRIDGET JONES

Bridget: "This is one occasion for genuinely tiny knickers."

Arabella had arranged to meet Tommy close to home so she didn't have to travel far. She was in such a rush she ran out of the house, barely looking in the mirror and felt like a terrible mother for leaving Lily with a babysitter.

Arabella, walking to the restaurant, suddenly remembered that she hadn't shaved her legs! Well, that wasn't very smart.

Tommy looked across at Arabella and grinned. "I thought you were beautiful when I first met you. I couldn't believe that you'd be interested in me."

Arabella was stunned. Tommy leant over to kiss her. God this was fun!

Oh please don't touch my legs, please don't touch my legs, she thought.

Tommy kissed her again. Her insides turned inside out. She felt great, the second glass of champagne probably partly responsible.

"I'd like to see you again if possible?" Tommy whispered in her ear.

"Okay," she answered far too quickly. Arabella prayed the floor would open and swallow her up. Tommy laughed, kissing her again.

He walked her home like a true gentleman. Arabella said goodnight and she went inside, alone. Arabella, now somewhat tipsy, logged onto her blog. She posted:

"I've found love and he is yummy with a very good bottom. Much better than Mark's, that's for sure."

She fell asleep, oblivious.

Arabella awoke to a string of texts. *"I cannot believe you! The whole world doesn't need to know what you're doing. I'm coming over to visit. You are obviously not fit enough to look after Lily, I'm bringing Betty."*

Oh bugger!

Arabella vaguely recalled typing away on her blog last night, but she didn't remember what she had written. What was Mark talking about? It couldn't have been that bad, surely? Okay, let's see... Arabella found the "dreaded" post and laughed out loud! Okay, yes it was a stupid thing to do but it was also kind of funny!

Naughty Arabella! No more drunk-blogging!

But Mark was clearly overreacting. Why was he even reading it? His ego had taken a bruising and now he was being dramatic, again. Arabella refused to apologize. *One tipsy post does not equate to bad parenting, Mark.*

Arabella immediately booked an appointment to go the hairdressers to make herself feel better. She loved going there, her safe haven. She sat under the dryer, writing her blog, answering texts and emails, bombarded by Mark every few minutes about dates for him to come out. He was now obsessed, like a bull in a China shop.

She picked up a gossip magazine. So many actors and actresses were getting divorced. She wondered how they dealt with annoying exes.

Bing. Text message from Mark.

"Who are you seeing?" He actually sounded jealous.

"None of your business," she replied. This line of questioning was starting to annoy her.

Bing. Another text.

"I'm coming over next week. Clear your schedule, I want to see Lily."

She sat bolt upright, banging her head on the dryer. Mark was trying to invade her happy place, dammit! She remembered Lily.

"I don't think this would be the best time to bring Betty."

Silence.

"Lily has had to deal with so much and it's too soon."

Silence.

"Betty is part of my life now, Arabella, and Lily will have to deal with that at some time.

Thank God for that, Arabella thought. But she still needed to prepare Lily for the inevitable, the new sibling.

Other than the news of Mark's imminent arrival, it was an incredible week. Lily was picked for a lead role in a popular TV show and Arabella had been asked to present her own agony aunt talk show on a major network. Hot A-list actors were throwing themselves at her and currently, there was a potential book deal in the works. Okay, it wasn't THAT marvellous but she hoped she would at least have things to tell Mark when he arrived. Her current mantra was "be kind to your ex-husband, especially when he's acting like a toddler."

She spent the week making sure the little house was in order. Arabella had put off telling Lily that Daddy was coming over, in case his plans suddenly changed last minute. However, as he was arriving the next day, she had no choice.

Arabella stroked Lily's head.

"Lily, mummy's got something to tell you."

"Are you going to marry Tommy?" she asked eagerly.

"No, my darling, definitely not, although…" Arabella smiled.

"What mummy?"

"Daddy is arriving tomorrow, just for a quick visit to say hi."

Lily remained silent

"Then I will make sure I'm unavailable." Lily mimicked trying to sound terribly grown up.

Arabella was at a loss for words. Lily's schedule was pretty free for the next few days, so lying to Mark might prove difficult.

"OK my darling, let's discuss it in the morning."

Arabella closed Lily's door and poured herself a small glass of white wine. She was ashamed to say she needed a little Dutch courage as of now.

"I am strong. I am courageous," she muttered to herself. "Please universe, give me the strength to help Lily get through this week." Arabella looked up at the night sky, marveling at its beauty. She felt better already.

ROMEO AND JULIET

Romeo: "What's here? Poison? Drunk all and left no friendly drops to help me after."

The next morning, Arabella dropped Lily off at a friend's and drove to the airport to collect Mark. She would use this time alone with him to discuss Lily. She felt bizarrely emotional but couldn't understand why. She was in a different place, she felt more confident, and things were recently starting to take off for her and Lily.

Whilst waiting for Mark she took herself off quickly to the toilet and there in front of her was the reason why she felt like this. Great, that time of the month. It was her mission to keep it together for the next few days. She could not and would not be needlessly emotional! Her sanity depended on it.

I'm here. Mark texted.

Breathe, Arabella breathe. Get ready, It's Showtime!

She spotted Mark looking less like his normal self. In fact, he looked awful. His hair was tinged grey, he'd lost weight and he had dark circles under his eyes, He looked strained. She knew this wasn't a competition, but he looked a little shocked when he laid eyes on her. Arabella had become a rejuvenated person in LA. She was tanned, slimmer than before and her hair was a brilliant blonde. She felt a million feet tall.

They got into the car, where a gaping silence threatened to swallow them both whole.

"Nice Beetle." Mark touched the interior of the car. Arabella wasn't sure if he was being sarcastic but she refused to take the bait.

"Yeah, it's a great fit for Lily and I." *What about your new Mercedes,* she thought. "And it drives well."

"How's Lily?" he asked.

"She's great! She's grown up so much since we moved out here."

Mark nodded.

"So where are you staying?" Arabella asked.

"Just up the street from you. If you don't mind dropping me off while I put down my bags, I can come back to yours to see Lily."

"Oh, I don't think tonight's a good idea," Arabella said.

"Why not?" Mark roared.

"She doesn't want to see you. I'm doing my best to convince her."

"What, is she still blaming me? You need to take responsibility for this too, you know. It wasn't all me."

Which part was she responsible for, Arabella wondered. The having sex with another woman? The lying about it for months? The divorce? Arabella chose her words carefully.

"She's a child, she needs time."

"I know, I get it, okay," Mark said, defeated.

The car grew silent once again.

"I've missed you a bit you know."

Huh? Arabella was not prepared for this admission at all.

"I see," was all Arabella could say.

Something didn't quite sit right with Arabella. She didn't trust Mark as far as she could throw him. And throwing him was something she'd considered often. Especially out of the moving car.

"I'll come by and collect you in the morning and you can pop in and say hi to Lily."

After dropping Mark off at the hotel, Arabella felt a sense of relief knowing she could go back to her lovely little cozy cottage.

When Arabella told her friends about Mark's arrival they arranged a Facetime session to give her support for the rest of his visit. They had apparently been keeping up with the Mark and Betty gossip.

"Now don't believe anything he says," Alice told her.

"Betty will have told him what to do and say, so don't trust him. He will want to please Betty all the time and only has her interests in mind," Jen added.

Nicki ended with, "Promise us you'll call to let us know what's going on."

Their session was suddenly over as a storm back in the UK cut the power off. Arabella certainly didn't miss the weather.

Lily was tucked up safely asleep. She thanked Charlotte for taking care of Lily and lay down. She too, fell into a deep slumber.

Every day started with:

"But Mummy, you promised, we could have a dog."

Arabella knew she had to address the matter soon, but first, she had more pressing matters to attend to.

"We can talk about that later this week, but now we have to talk about Daddy."

"Where's Daddy? Are we seeing him? I don't want to." Lily seemed anxious.

It was only 7.30 a.m. and Arabella knew Lily needed calming down. She told her to get dressed so they could take their usual walk to Starbucks.

As they walked past the shops towards the coffee shop, Arabella stopped. She was convinced she had just seen Mark coming out of a local yoga studio. No, it couldn't be him, surely? Arabella tried to calm herself down, unsure why this upset her so. Mark could do whatever he wanted. But he was only here for one week and already displayed signs of his selfishness. It was all about him. Maybe Arabella needed some time to go to yoga.

OK, not yoga, more like a visit to the nail bar.

"Mummy, what's the matter?" Lily asked.

"Nothing Lily, mummy is just being silly."

She wished she had another watermelon to throw. Not in to the sea, but at Mark's head.

She messaged him and watched as he looked at the message.

"Where do you want to meet? Sorry I know it's early. Are you awake yet?"

"Just woken up, will meet you in Mason's coffee house," he responded.

What a liar! Why didn't he just admit to going to the yoga studio? Another of his secrets, nothing had changed. Maybe he had secretly brought Betty over. She didn't trust him at all. Maybe Betty was actually going to surprise them all and be at the coffee shop.

"Let's come back for a coffee later with Daddy, I want to go for a walk," Arabella said.

Lily had no idea what was happening but Arabella grabbed her and they ran to the other side of the road.

"Mummy, what are we doing?"

"We are playing hide and seek," she thought quickly.

"But we are hiding in the same place."

"Yep, it's a new game."

Arabella started trailing Mark, wondering if he was even staying where he said he was staying. Arabella and Lily were not exactly wearing inconspicuous clothing either, with bright white jeans and bright blue tops.

Hopefully Mark wouldn't notice them. Arabella made sure they kept their distance.

"Mummy this isn't very much fun," Lily whined.

"Yes, it is, I'm having lots of fun."

"No, it isn't," Lily whinged.

"Just one more road, okay Lily?"

But Lily stood firm.

"I'll get you a treat."

Lily perked up at the sound of the word "treat."

They followed Mark back up the street only to find themselves at his house, the house she had dropped him off at last night. No sign of Betty.

Tom Cruise in *Mission Impossible* she was not.

She made Lily walk back to Mason's coffee house and they sat and waited. No-one looked like Betty. As usual, Mark was late but seemed genuinely pleased to see Lily.

"I've got you a present, Lily. Now you don't have to keep it, but I bought you something when I went away on holiday."

Arabella knew which holiday he was talking about. They had gone away with Betty's family and she heard via the village grapevine that he was going to propose to Betty next time they travelled there.

Mark was acting like such a big shot, blabbering to all and sundry about how influential, powerful and rich his new in-laws were, that Arabella's mother Sarah wanted to find out for herself. She was concerned about Lily being involved with a questionable family. She, of course, could smell a rat immediately. She said any dirt she had uncovered would be kept "just in case." Arabella had no idea what her mother meant by that, but seeing as she had done very well in all five of her divorces she trusted her opinion in these matters.

"I have a file my darling. Just in case we need evidence."

Lily looked at the present. "Thank you, I will open it later."

The mood had become rather somber and Arabella tried to liven things up. "So why don't we all go shopping? Or we could all go to the beach?"

Mark looked hopeful and Arabella looked at Lily as if to say, 'come on let's give him a chance'. Lily didn't respond, which Arabella took as a yes. Well, it wasn't a no!

They got in the car and drove to the local shopping mall, Arabella still making small talk.

"Gosh, I remember when mummy and daddy first took you to buy a pair of shoes."

Lily's face brightened.

"Really?" Lily asked.

"Yes, you were adorable and wanted a pair like Dorothy in *The Wizard of Oz*."

Mark started to join in too and before long they were chatting about lots of little things that they all remembered and shared, happy thoughts transforming the conversation.

They moved onto Lily's favorite topic, Mark and Arabella's wedding.

Lily had been a bridesmaid and loved hearing about the time she ran down the aisle shouting, "No!"

As Mark spoke about the wedding, Arabella thought perhaps she saw a tiny flash of doubt cross his face. Was he second guessing his life with Betty? Arabella really didn't need this in her life right now. She was feeling settled and happy with her new-found freedom.

"Do you remember our first kiss?" Mark asked Arabella.

Where is he going with this line of questioning, she wondered.

Arabella thought back to it, it had been wonderful. Mark had fancied her so much.

Mark placed his hand on Arabella's. "Mummy was my first proper love."

Arabella was stumped. What was going on? There must be a reason why he was suddenly being so nice?

They had an amazing day shopping and recalling the good ol' times. Mark didn't even answer his texts from Betty. It was just the three of them again. Lily was so happy. She seemed to warm to Mark and they connected over books she was reading at the time.

"I'm glad you're into all this stuff, darling. Maybe you're taking after your dad," he joked.

Arabella kept her mouth firmly shut. If anyone in the family was an avid reader and had been for years, it was her. *Must not be petty, must not be petty,* she chanted under her breath.

On the drive back, Lily fell asleep in the car. They both lifted her up and took her inside. It felt odd, like they were a family again, as if Mark had never left.

"Let's try and have a day like this every day," Mark whispered to her.

Arabella watched Mark leave. She didn't know what to make of the whole situation. But she knew one thing for sure, she didn't trust him at all.

Even though she desperately wanted to.

JERRY MAGUIRE

Dorothy: "You had me at 'hello.'"

It was their last day together, Mark, Arabella and Lily had had a wonderful week as a family. Arabella couldn't believe how it had whizzed by. Arabella had offered to take Mark to the airport that evening so she told him to leave his bag in her car so they wouldn't have to pick it up later.

Lily and Mark had wanted to nip into the shops and Arabella said she would wait in the car so that they could have some daddy-daughter alone time.

Her phone rang, it was Mark. "I'm getting something for Lily but I need my passport as ID to use my credit card. Is it in the front part of my bag"?

Arabella searched through but couldn't find it. She lifted a notebook out of his bag and shook it in case it was hidden. Some papers fell out.

"Don't worry, it's here in my pocket," he told her.

Before she had time to respond, Mark was gone. She was going to put the papers back when she saw her name and Lily's scribbled across the page.

Hug her when you see her, discuss the house money, talk about her earnings. 2015 Spain, St Bart's, Skiing, 2016 South Africa, LA, skiing. Find evidence that Lily isn't being cared for properly, search for any evidence surrounding Arabella's relationships.

What was this list, Arabella wondered? Some kind of weird shopping list?

Oh, I see!

It finally dawned on Arabella. Mark had written a list on how to behave this week and what he needed to say to Arabella and what information he needed to take back to the UK. It was all pre-planned! Lily and Arabella were on his tick sheet.

Further reading of the notebook revealed that he was away on holiday nearly every month and that he had recently taken out another loan. So that's how he was able to propose to Betty and afford to buy her a very large engagement ring! He had everything perfectly planned out.

She felt like a fool. He had been trying to gather information about Arabella and Lily to build up a case for court. He wasn't wanting to become friends, he wasn't wanting to spend time with Lily. She had mistaken his friendship this week as something genuine. Tears of anger and frustration poured out of her. She had so badly wanted to believe he was over here for Lily. She quickly put the notebook back, Composed herself and waited till they arrived back.

"All okay?" he asked when they returned.

"Yep, just perfect, thank you," Arabella eyed Mark totally differently, seeing through his new mask of deceit.

At least she now knew where she stood. He had been playing her this whole time. He could never be trusted.

She took Lily to Charlotte's and told her to stay there whilst she took Daddy to the airport.

"Bye Daddy." Although Lily had fun with Mark, she didn't seem too concerned by Mark's departure.

"Okay my darling, I will see you soon I hope." Mark hugged and kissed her.

"Yep."

And that was it, off she went to play.

Mark got back in the car.

"I really miss her you know, everyone does."

Arabella refused to be drawn into this conversation. Instead, she pulled out the decree absolute paperwork from her bag.

"Here, I've signed them."

Mark was stunned. He hadn't expected Arabella to actually hand the divorce papers over. He looked uncomfortable.

"It's fine if you need more time?"

"Nope, I'm all good."

They didn't talk the whole way to the airport. When they arrived, Mark grabbed his bags and turned to Arabella. "You know, I am sorry about everything."

"Bye Mark." She barely looked at him and drove away.

Arabella was officially done with Mark. She didn't cry. She didn't even want to think about him. She turned the music up, blasting out her favourite tunes as she took the scenic road back along the coast.

The following week was a whirlwind of activities as Lily went back and forth from auditions to filming. At one of the auditions, Arabella let Lily go in by herself, but this time she told Arabella that the director wanted to ask her a few questions.

"Hi, I'm Simon," he introduced himself.

"Arabella. Pleased to meet you"

"Lily is very talented and we would love her to be in our commercial. It's shooting this weekend. Is she available?"

"Yes, I think we can fit it in," Arabella answered.

"Do you need to let anyone know? Your husband?" he continued.

"Oh no, I'm not married," she quickly replied.

"Your boyfriend? Partner?" Arabella didn't know directors were so involved in the talent's family members.

"No, I don't have a boyfriend either." She said blushing slightly.

"Oh."

Simon grinned, looking pleased with himself.

"Well then that's a date," he said.

A what? Arabella felt like somehow she'd been roped into an actual date. Was she imagining things? She stared at him, waiting for an answer.

"I mean a date for Lily to be filmed. I will forward the location and times with my contact details."

Yeah right, she thought. She wasn't born yesterday.

"Well done darling, you got a job and mummy might have got a date." Arabella laughed with confidence. It had been a while since her last date with Tommy. Arabella had told him she couldn't see him whilst Mark had been over and that once Mark left she would text him. As luck would have it, Tommy had been given the lead in a film. He would be leaving for Vancouver to shoot for four months. But if she ever wanted a weekend away she could visit him anytime.

Arabella knew her dirty weekends away were only going to happen in her dreams for the moment. She was fine with that.

Being on set was a whole new experience for Arabella. Lily's filming weekend went incredibly well, with Simon involving Arabella in all aspects of the shooting, explaining how everything worked. Simon was so encouraging and by the end of it, they felt like they had known each other for years. Arabella hadn't realized how much fun this "set stuff" was.

Simon also showed a huge interest in Arabella's blog. They spoke about her writing ideas, and films she liked, and Simon appeared to take a real interest in her. It was fun to talk about something so totally different to other areas in her life.

Arabella continued to see Simon after Lily's weekend of filming. A picnic on the beach, a trip to the movie theatre, a night at a concert on Santa Monica Pier. Simon had built up enough courage to invite her to a screening of his film the following weekend, playing out of town. She hesitated, worrying about Lily. Charlotte immediately offered to have her though, so Arabella thought why not.

Simon was the perfect gentleman, he even thought to arrange separate rooms in the hotel where they were staying.

This was the first time she was going away without Lily.

"Don't you worry yourself," comforted Charlotte. "Lily and I will have a wonderful time together. Go and enjoy yourself."

Arabella tried on all her outfits and started packing. Once more she felt like Rene Russo from the *Thomas Crown Affair*, where she was going to be taken on a private plane to an island where they would sit by a fire and go down to the beach and she would throw a Monet in the fire. Okay not quite, but she liked the first part.

She would turn up and he would rip her dress off her and they would make love all night long and then order room service all weekend. Or maybe they would head off on his Harley and investigate the countryside.

What was she thinking? Just to even be taken away was a treat, as she had been working so hard on her blog and catering for Lily's needs.

Her bag was packed with four dresses and two pairs of shoes. As she was getting ready, Lily looked concerned.

"Mummy, you will come back won't you?"

"Of course my darling. I couldn't possibly live without you. You're the most important person in mummy's whole world. You know that right? This trip is important for mummy. When you get older, you'll understand."

"Well mummy, I want you to have a really good time," Lily grinned.

"I hope I'm taking the right clothes," Arabella muttered out loud.

"Mummy, you look beautiful in everything you wear," Lily said, whilst trying on the remainder of Arabella's clothes because she thought this was helpful. The tiny bedroom was now covered with the left-over clothes, dresses, shoes, trousers, and tops.

Arabella didn't know what to expect from Simon. Were they just friends or was he going to want to take her right then and there on the red carpet? Or on the back row whilst his movie was playing?

"And the award for the best film goes to Mr. Simon Bucks. If Mr. Bucks would like to come and receive his award."

Silence.

"Mr. Bucks?"

Still nothing. Arabella, mid-kiss, realized Simon was being called.

"Simon, they want you!" she pushed him away.

Arabella quickly adjusted her top so no-one would know what they had been doing in the back of the theatre.

"Come up with me. You're the love of my life and I couldn't have done any of this without you, Arabella. Arabella!" he begged.

"Mummy, Arabella, you did that thing again where you look like you are on another planet," Lily looked at her mother.

"Sorry darling, I was just thinking about the…....."

Before she could finish her sentence, Lily interrupted her.

"Simon, you love him don't you mummy? Simon and Mummy up a tree kissing," she teased. Arabella threw the cushion at her playfully.

"Mummy don't worry. He will like you whatever you wear."

"How did you get so wise?" Arabella asked.

"Because I have you as a mummy."

Arabella leant over and kissed her beautiful daughter. She was wise for one so young.

"So what about this dress?" she held up a green ensemble.

"Mummy, you look like a princess. Why couldn't you have been a fairy godmother because then I could have been a fairy?"

Lily often asked unusual questions like this. Just last week she had discussed magic.

"I wish I was magic. I've tried really hard to do exactly what they tell you to do on *Once Upon a Time,*" she told Arabella in a very serious tone.

She was referring to her favorite show. Arabella could see why, she often vacillated between the evil queen and Snow White herself.

Arabella eyed herself in the mirror. She was quite okay with what she could see. She felt in a good place and was looking forward to the trip.

"Time for bed. Good night Lily, I love you to the moon and back," Arabella said.

"What's your first favorite way to sleep?" Lily asked.

"With you," Arabella nuzzled Lily's cheek with her nose.

"Okay mummy. Goodnight," she said, comforted.

"Night my darling, I will see you after the weekend."

Arabella closed the bedroom door just as Charlotte arrived and that was it, off she went yonder, to greater plains.

GHOST

Molly: "I love you, I really love you."

The airport was absolute chaos that night. Arabella bought a coffee and felt lost with only herself to look after. She never really took time out for herself so she hoped she knew how to act like a normal single adult.

No need to panic, Arabella!

A text from Simon put her immediately at ease.

"Can't wait to see you later."

Her phone buzzed. It was a text from Alice telling her in no uncertain terms that she had "better go and have a good time and she wanted all the details". Arabella smiled to herself. Most of all she wanted to be able to have an inspiring, grown-up weekend.

Her seat number was called and she stood in line.

"Can I get you a drink, madam?" the steward asked as she sat down on the plane.

"I would love a glass of champagne, please. I think I deserve it."

As the flight took off Arabella began updating her blog. She had at least an hour before they landed.

When she arrived, Simon collected her. It was like a perfect movie scene, but this time it was actually happening. It was real. He was there, waiting for her.

"I've got a surprise for you," Simon whispered in the limo, he leant over and gave her a gift.

"Now please don't think I'm being presumptuous but I saw this and thought of you." It was an emerald ring. A costume piece, but it didn't matter. The shape of a spider. How many times had she asked Mark, dropping hints about how she would love an emerald ring, her birth stone? A ring that symbolized their love and represented what they meant to each other. But it had never happened. Here she was, handed one out the blue, when she couldn't even remember mentioning it to him once.

"What? How did you know? Thank you." Arabella was overwhelmed with gratitude.

"It was your blog, you wrote about wanting an emerald ring in one of your blogs."

He actually read her blogs.

This was going to be a weekend to remember.

The hotel was magical. A boutique hotel. They both went into their separate rooms. She quickly changed into the outfit Lily had suggested and they left almost immediately. On arrival at the movie theatre they sat and watched Simon's film and he reached over and tenderly held Arabella's hand.

When the final credits rolled, Simon grabbed Arabella and said, "Let's leave now before I get stopped by the paparazzi."

But it was too late, the press were outside the theatre and started to take photos.

"Sorry about this," he said.

"It's fine," she mouthed.

He pulled her towards the red carpet, seemingly proud to have her by her side. She couldn't believe that she was here, only a year and three months since that fateful day when she discovered those messages and photos between Mark and Betty. At this moment, right now, the world was pretty special.

AMERICAN BEAUTY

Lester: "I feel like I've been in a coma for the past twenty years and I'm just now waking up."

Another couple of months had passed without a hitch and Simon and Arabella were officially seeing each other. Arabella had applied for her and Lily's working visas to stay in LA. There had been a big discussion about whether they should extend their stay in LA. Arabella couldn't bear to go back and face Mark and Betty. Lily was flourishing, working hard, several auditions a week. A couple of commercials under her belt. They still didn't have the dog. Arabella needed more time to recover. Her blog was taking off and more and more hits were coming in each day. People were commenting and reading about her new-found life. There appeared to be a group of single Mums who were wanting to change their lives too, so Arabella had found her perfect audience.

Arabella was developing as a fiction writer as well and Simon had suggested a screenwriting course to grow her skills. Simon was still on the scene, he was being as charming and lovely as ever. Arabella wasn't ready to commit to a serious relationship but things were heading in the right direction for them both. She was pleasantly optimistic.

Writing had really been a type of therapy for her. Everything felt right, even though Arabella had in the back of her mind that she did have to face the inevitable. The divorce was due any day. She knew she would have to face her fear and fly back to the UK to finalise financials.

It didn't need thinking about now though.

This was the future, right here and now. She looked down at her emerald ring and thought to herself:

There's no place like home, there's no place like home.

THE END

NEXT BOOK: HOLLYWOOD'S BEST KEPT SECRET.

Another year filled with life's curveballs. Divorce court, a baby, a wedding. Arabella woke with a jolt. Had that been an awful dream? She sat up with a start and looked around her bedroom in Beverly Hills, her eyes searching the room. She stretched her hand across the bed. Simon wasn't there. Simon had disclosed all of this new information over supper last night. Simon had managed to mislead her for a whole year. Damn it, now who was the fool!

ABOUT THE AUTHOR

Elizabeth has always been a writer, it just took some life changing moments to bring this to the forefront of her everyday life. She first started with her blog- *Divorcee, Daughter and Dog.* Then it all seemed to flow; the screenplays, the children's books and the adult fiction.

Her life has often been likened to that of a movie and so what better industry to be in than the movies. She is a writer/director and is currently working on several feature films that will be released in 2018.

Elizabeth lives with her dog Chai, (because it's her favourite drink) and her actress daughter Isabella, whom she home-schools (that's the daughter, not the dog) in a small beach cottage in Hermosa Beach.

Elizabeth believes in making the most of life's opportunities and works 24/7 wanting her daughter to understand that hard work and dedication can make your dreams come true. Life can throw some curveballs at you, but they make you grow. Her pet hate is when someone says they are going to do something, but don't do it.

She loves the sun, eating sushi and enjoys travelling the world.

Gerard Butler once told her she had a "lovely bottom".

45985771R00130

Printed in Poland
by Amazon Fulfillment
Poland Sp. z o.o., Wrocław